Time 10:31. Cityside released rockets and biobombs as scheduled against Landsend from Sector Seven this morning. Conquer-kill count up from yesterday it is believed. Work hard. Work wins. Work hard. Work wins.

The factclock fell silent.

Villane picked up his Production Report and recited into the datafix. "Virulence of new strain point four hundred two. Room for improvement. Succeeding generations expected to increase in kill capacity. Recommend airborne delivery and dispersal to insure sufficient decimation and to—"

Villane vomited. It happened suddenly and without warning. His chest heaved once, twice, calmed. The sudden storm that had buffeted his body billowed away in dark silence, leaving him befouled of body but incredibly clear of mind. He looked around him at the laboratory as if seeing it for the first time, remembered the inhuman voice of the factclock ticking off the Conquer-kill count and heard the ominous silence that swirled up from the innocent looking test tubes where painful death lurked waiting.

BELMONT SELECT SCIENCE FICTION

LEO P. KELLEY

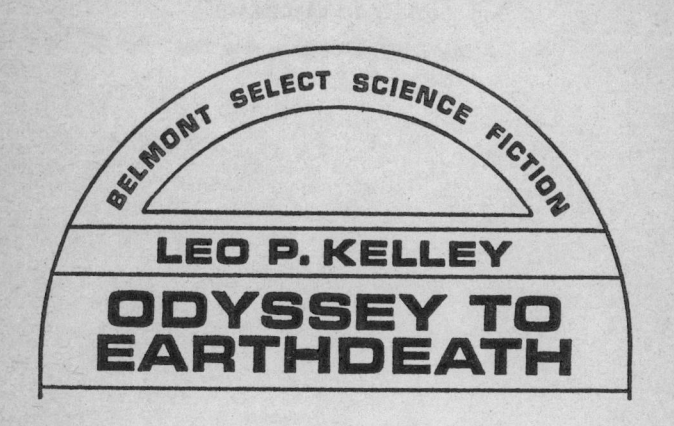

ODYSSEY TO EARTHDEATH

BELMONT BOOKS ● NEW YORK CITY

ODYSSEY TO EARTHDEATH

A BELMONT BOOK—November 1968

Published by
Belmont Productions, Inc.
1116 First Avenue, New York, N.Y. 10021

Copyright © 1968 by Leo P. Kelley. All rights reserved.

PRINTED IN THE UNITED STATES OF AMERICA

Where is joy in
The killing of kinsmen?

                Bhagavad-Gita

PART ONE

The Folk

THE NEEDLE slipped into the man's bulging vein. Phillip Villane watched the blood flow up to fill the syringe he held in his right hand like too little time running out, away. Mechanically, he withdrew the syringe from his assistant's arm and, with his left hand, pressed cotton to the wound left by the single tooth of the needle. He waved the man away.

When he was alone, Villane proceeded with his experiment. He prepared the slide, adjusted the microscope and bent down over it. Only the tense line of his jaw and the twitching muscle in his cheek betrayed his uneasiness. There beneath his eye swam the red and white corpuscles, unaware of the impending battle in which they were about to take part. He raised his head and drew the culture tray toward him. He added a drop from the bacterial culture to the red stain on the slide and with a painful curiosity bent his head to the lens of the microscope once again to watch the battle begin.

The bacilli were at first defensive as the body's warriors, the white knights hidden in the red blood, rose to do battle. But soon the tide turned as Villane had known it would. Not for nothing had the deadly bacilli been bred down through scores of brief and ever more virulent generations. Not for mere amusement had their deadliness been cultivated, nursed and coddled like a new species of evil green rose. Squirming beneath Villane's anxious eyes, the bacilli attacked and killed as they had been bred to do. Death, reliable and efficient, wriggled on the slide under the unfeeling eye of the microscope and swarmed invisible in the shallow culture tray resting on the laboratory table.

Villane raised his head as the paradox screamed like a severed mandrake in the tangle of his mind. He had succeeded in creating death to preserve life—the life of Cityside and its inhabitants; the death of the profane *others* out there in Landsend beyond the heat fields encircling Cityside and sealing it off from any contact, any attack by the Landsenders. Was it true then, he asked himself, that death was necessary to life? Perhaps. But still he wondered about alternatives—and found only further paradoxes. A relative peace existed only because of the weapons stockpiled in the secret arsenals of Cityside. Life could be preserved against the threat of the enemy in Landsend only by the skillful creation of neater and more intricate ways of delivering death to that enemy.

Villane found himself wondering again what Earth War Three had really been like. He had heard it whispered about and he had nightmared about it for nearly all of his twenty-seven years. Every Citysider had. It had ended over sixty years ago, in the year 1981. Among the survivors were those who had banded together for mutual protection and built Cityside which now sprawled over most of what had once been the eastern seaboard of the United States. They had sealed it off from the rest of the world—what was left of it—with heat fields and armed it to the towers against those who even now might be dreaming of Earth War Four.

Why, Villane marveled, I have known only peace during my lifetime. Like a playful ghost, the ridiculous laughter flowed from his mouth. He stifled it at once with stiff commands to his tongue, teeth and lips. Sobering, he reminded himself that they were not to be trusted, those *others* out there in Landsend. Why, everyone had been told and told, they wanted Earth War Four as the mamba wants flesh in its poisonous fangs. How was it possible, Villane wondered, for Landsenders to want what no sane man should ever want, not even in the fiery depths of his most fevered dreams? He didn't know.

The siren-shrill voice of the factclock derailed his train of thought:

Time 10:31. Cityside released rockets and biobombs as scheduled against Landsend from Sector Seven this morning. Conquer-kill count up from yesterday it is believed. Work hard. Work wins. Work hard. Work wins.

The factclock fell silent.

Villane picked up his Production Report and went to his desk in a corner of the room. He entered figures in his quota column and then recited into the datafix: "Virulence of new strain point four hundred two. Room for improvement. Succeeding generations expected to increase in kill capacity. Recommend airborne delivery and dispersal to insure sufficient decimation and to—"

Villane vomited. It happened suddenly and without warning and he saw it happening, felt the warm viscous mass flood his mouth and spill out onto his uniform and he did not care. The Production Report fell from his hands to the metal floor. His chest heaved once, twice, calmed. The sudden storm that had buffeted his body billowed away in dark silence, leaving him befouled of body but incredibly clear of mind. He looked around him at the laboratory as if seeing it for the first time, remembered the inhuman voice of the factclock ticking off the Conquer-kill count and heard the ominous silence that swirled up from the innocent looking test tubes where painful death lurked waiting.

The voice of the datafix: "All? All? If all, sign please."

And then, from the lost countries of earlier days came the half-remembered words to taunt him. They were unreal and nonfactual but then so was imagination, he reminded himself. With a perverse glee, he told the datafix, "No, that is not all. I am not finished."

What were the words? He remembered and told the datafix, "There was a time when all the world did seem to me to be appareled in celestial light."

The red light of the datafix flashed ominously, warning of information mix.

"Correction," he said. "There *never* was a time when all the world did seem to me to be appareled in celestial light."

Sadly, he switched off the datafix and went into the cleanroom. He stood before the huge mirror, his hands hanging at his sides, studying himself as he might have studied a stranger. His body, all lean meat and raw bones. Black hair that fringed the high creased plain of his forehead and lay thick and low on his neck just above his shoulders. Eyes that were neither blue nor green but something in between. A squarish skull sprouting the normal appurtenances—two ears, a minor mountain of a nose, chin, thin lips. His now filthy white uniform.

Almost joyfully, he tore it off and turned on the steam spray to cleanse himself. He raised his head and let the steam stream into his mouth, wishing it could riot through him and burn away all the horrors that lurked in the electrochemical factory beneath the bone of his skull that would be with him until he died.

Died.

He didn't want to die. But neither did he want to live he had suddenly realized as he watched the microscopic battle and listened dutifully to the Conquer-kill count on the factclock. Not like this. A fine dilemma. Well, he decided, I will live. I will not die. But I will throw down my banner, withdraw from the lists and let whatever might happen as a result of my traitorous act happen.

He stepped out of the steam spray and stretched as if to tear down the white ceiling high above his head. If I cannot practice life, he thought, I will at least no longer manufacture death.

The monitor on the cleanroom wall glowed into life.

The face of the Director of the Life Laboratory appeared and his voice crackled, "There you are, Villane. Technician meeting. Report at once to the Main Mall."

Villane shook his head. "No," he said.

The Director squinted and repeated his command more firmly this time.

"No," Villane said a second time.

The monitor abruptly went dark.

Naked and without fear, Villane waited for them to come for him.

He was a giant jelly of a man dressed in a red robe, its cowl covering his shaved head, and black leather boots that reached to his knees. As he sat in his seat aboard the carveyor carrying him through the sterile streets beneath the gleaming towers of Cityside, his flesh jiggled on his bones, his eyes saw everything and only his lips smiled. He looked a little like one of the immense figures in an ancient amusement park that giggled electronically and slapped its sides in mechanical mirth as its wires hummed and its relay switches clicked precisely.

He was Supreme Priestman Simon Pume. He was the commander of Cityside's omnipresent Priestmen who, as individuals, represented the economical and felicitous fusion of the priest and police castes of Cityside. Thus, a single, efficient, elite group of men not only created and defined Cityside's morality but also rigidly enforced it.

Pume was on his way, for the last time, he hoped, to the Disposal Depot located in Cityside's Sector Two beyond which lay the dreaded and dangerous territory of Landsend.

People sat quietly in their seats on the carveyor which carried them along like a human river moving beneath a thick mantle of winter ice—smoothly, silently. They wore the white uniforms, some of them, of workers in the Life Laboratory. On their raised podiums above the gliding flocks of aeroautos jetting along on their cushions of air, stood the yellow-robed and booted Priestmen directing traffic diligently.

Pume listened with pleasure.

"Good morning, glory!" brayed the Priestman at the next corner. "All's swell that works well!" Smiling, smiling.

The Priestman received stiff, practiced smiles in return from the people aboard the carveyor and in their aeroautos as they thought of their jobs and of another day to be gotten through somehow. Desperate thoughts, dry as dust in their minds, blowing this way and that, seeking escape through their ears or between their teeth.

"The best is," sang the Priestman at the next corner as Pume stepped off the carveyor.

Pume saw the citizen near him suddenly stop in his tracks and begin to shudder convulsively, his body shaking in an unrehearsed gavotte. He saw the Priestman raise his airtube to his mouth and blow into it. The pellet flew out of the airtube, struck the man and entered his quaking body. In mere moments, the tranquilagent it contained dissolved in the man's bloodstream and he gradually stopped shaking. He straightened and ran a hand through his hair, shook his head once, fixed a false smile on his face and walked on like a soldier who has remembered a war to be won.

Suddenly, Pume's eyes narrowed. Were those tears in the eyes of that Life Labber, that thin girl with the gleaming black hair just ahead? He quickened his pace. Danger, said his brain. Watch out, said his heart. He considered summoning the Priestman to his side but decided he would be able to handle this matter himself.

Coming abreast of the girl, he fell into step beside her. "Nice day," he said too loudly.

"Ruth Cameron, Life Labber, Tier Twenty, Project Death Development," the girl replied automatically.

Pume peered at her intently. Perhaps it was only her makeup glistening in the sun. Yes, that could be it. But was it? "I am not interested in your name," he said sharply.

The girl turned, her step missing a beat. "Oh," she

said. "Oh, sorry, I—" Then, seeing who her companion was, she said, "Good morning, sir."

"Your eyes, my dear—?"

"The wind. Just the wind." She wiped a hand across her face and when it had fallen once again to her side, she managed a bright smile that dazzled Pume despite the hazy suspicions that were dragging at the muscles of his mouth.

"Save Cityside!" Pume declared.

"Down with Landsend," the girl responded, making the safety sign by waving her right hand in front of her in a gesture like that of a child rejecting his cereal.

Pume watched the girl vanish in the crowd. He walked on while the cheerfully chanted litany of the Priestmen flooded the morning air: *Live and let Landsend die. Look sharp! Do to Landsenders what Landsenders want to do to you! Look sharp!*

He snorted, thinking for what must have been the thousandth time that slogans were not enough. If you wanted to motivate people you had to give them something more than mere slogans. A little bread. A lot of circuses! Pume knew that all citizens had enough bread. The problem, simply stated, was circuses.

And that's where I come in and that's where it all has to start, he told himself. He was almost ready. He had conceived his idea during the meeting of the Council Committee three months ago. It had been John Detroy who had unwittingly struck the spark and Pume had watched it flame into life before his bemused eyes.

Detroy, Pume remembered, had been droning on for the better part of an hour, reciting statistics that revealed how much energy was required per microsecond to maintain the heat field surrounding Cityside and ticking off for the edification of his listeners the figures in the debit and credit columns of his quarterly budget-to-kill-ratio report.

"—simply thousands of man hours lost!" Detroy exclaimed, fussing among the papers littering the table in front of him. Like a lean mole, he burrowed among them and at last raised his head with a triumphant gleam in his eye. "Here," he said, tapping the paper with an immaculate fingernail. "Documented proof. A complete list. Names. Williams, Patterson, Aiello, Chee—"

"You needn't read us every name, John," said a thickset member of the Council wearily. "Just facsimilize the report and send each of us a copy."

Detroy cried, "But what I want to know is how we're going to prevent this rate of psych-sickness! Some of our best personnel arc victims. The strain of the Defense and Deterrence Effort, Allegiance Alerts—it's getting to be too much for a lot of us—them!"

"You're not suggesting, John, that we reduce the Bomb Buildup?" remarked the thickset Council member nervously. "Or that we eliminate Allegiance Alerts?"

"Certainly not!" Detroy snapped. "But figures don't lie and these figures tell a truth that makes me not only nervous but also scared. If this ratio continues, if we keep losing personnel—key ones, mind you—Cityside will become one huge human dump. There'll be no one left to maintain the heat field, no one to manufacture weaponry, no one to sell Survival Certificates—!"

"But percentagewise, we're still ahead of the game, aren't we?" someone asked.

Detroy pointed out in a so-there voice, "We admitted two hundred and eleven personnel to the Disposal Depot in the last quarter alone!"

Pume, flicked into keen awareness by the sharp arrows of argument flying about the room, listened intently.

Another Council member spoke. "Maybe we could assign a detachment of qualified meditechs to treat these psych-sicks. That is, of course, if the Defense and Deterrence people could spare them."

"And let production fall?" the man on his left asked in shocked tones. He shook his head and eyed his colleague suspiciously as if he thought that he too might be in the early stages of psych-sickness.

Detroy clapped his hands together impatiently. "Gentlemen, please! The first step is to define the problem. The second, to find a solution to the problem so defined.

Now I believe the problem is basically and fundamentally one of stress. Defense and Deterrence makes demands on us all. Some of us cope better than others. Those of us who can't cope get psych-sick. Why? Well, I for one think that these noncopers, for want of a better term, need a chance to relax, to unwind. They need, so to speak, a vacation."

Detroy's colleagues stared at him in disbelief, all except Simon Pume. In Pume's enterprising brain the first seedling of an idea was pushing through the soil of his synapses and growing quickly into a bright bloom of thought. But the others were shocked by the words Detroy had used, dangerous words, perhaps even treasonable words —*relax, unwind, vacation!*

"My good man," began the thickset Council member, seeming to speak for all of them, "my good man, you must realize that every one of us has to pull his weight and help guide our ship of state to safe harbor. Why, if we were to *relax* for an instant Landsenders would swarm over Cityside, topple its towers, defile its women and massacre its men. No, I say. And no again! It is unthinkable!" Just what was unthinkable the gentleman did not make perfectly clear but the nodding heads and clucking tongues seemed to say that everyone in the room agreed with him, whatever it was he had proposed or opposed.

Pume rose slowly. "May I say a word or two, gentlemen?"

Detroy said, "The Chair recognizes Supreme Priestman Pume."

"We live in grave and trying times," Pume began, trying his best to make the sheep that filled his eyes go away and let the men he knew were supposed to be there return.

The men bleated, "Hear, hear!" There was even a smattering of applause.

Pume continued sonorously, "Yes, grave and trying. And as I see it, some of our most devoted citizens are falling victims to uh, mental fatigue. Now before I go on, let me remind you that I scored 93.4% in our last Allegiance Alert."

"No one questions your loyalty, Priestman Pume," volunteered the man sitting nearest Pume.

Piously, Detroy, who fancied himself something of a poet, remarked, "Question rather that the sun should rise tomorrow than question the dedication and devotion of our most leading citizen. Excuse me, I mean most *learned* citizen."

"Well," Pume said, as he mentally sheared the wool from the figures before him, "the simple fact of the matter is that we have too little entertainment in our weary world. Landsend is to blame, of course," he added quickly. "But can we let Landsend insidiously force us to a state of inner collapse? Can we let these demons that stalk beyond the safety and civility of Cityside wreak such suffering on us as we seek only to preserve our glorious way of life? I ask you, gentlemen, can we allow this?"

Pume let the anticipated nos come and go on the air before him. He nursed the seedling in his brain while he spoke and what he asked for was time to evaluate this rich new growth and, like the careful gardener he intended to be, bring it bursting forth in full maturity. "Let me work on ways and means," Pume pleaded persuasively. "As I see it, the problem is simple but the solution —ah, the solution may be complex. I shall report back to you just as soon as I can. In the meantime, I ask you to consider the value of a bullet with no sane finger to release it and send it winging on its way."

A month later, Pume returned, having requested that the Council Committee meet in special session. Detroy called the meeting to order and then nodded to Pume.

"Man does not live by bombs alone," Pume intoned, seeking successfully to mystify his audience. "Yes, we all know the necessity of bombs. Without them, our life would be worthless. Landsend would destroy us. But bombs, I respectfully submit, are not enough. In addition, *circuses* are needed!"

Pume paused to let his message sail out like a paper

airplane to land in the minds of his hearers. He went on "We need circuses to lighten the hearts and lift the minds of our loyal and dedicated citizens."

"Froth and frivolity!" objected a Council member angrily. "First things first, I always say—"

"And second things second!" countered Pume. "It is this admitted froth and frivolity, the esteemed representative from Sector Six will agree, I trust, that will insure— to refer to my earlier analogy made at our last meeting —that the finger on the trigger and the brain behind it will have the strength and the will to *function!*"

"He's got something there," someone whispered in a tone thick with awe.

"Any objections?" Detroy asked. Seeing that there were none, he turned to Pume. "How do you propose to begin, Priestman Pume?"

"I propose," Pume said, "that we hold our circuses regularly and systematically for the benefit of all citizens of Cityside. Regularly, yes, and by that I mean every night. At midnight!"

"Midnight?" Detroy looked puzzled.

"This schedule will not interfere with the day duties of our citizens," Pume explained.

"But," a Council member protested, "won't that tend to tire and weaken our personnel if they spend night after night at circuses? Priestman, your plan seems to me to spell disaster in terms of a rising rate of susceptibility to psych-sickness."

"Not at all, not at all," Pume hastily assured his colleague. "Why, just think of the fun—the *fun,* I say—that a circus will bring to rejuvenate our citizens. What are a few hours of lost sleep compared with the riches they will reap during their brief respite from D & D and Allegiance Alerts."

"How do you propose to begin, Priestman Pume?" asked Detroy. "How, for example, will you staff your circus? How will you finance it?"

"If the Council will indulge me," Pume purred, "the matter of expenses, although not crucial, is important. I would like to request a small appropriation. Just enough to insure the success of our project. And permission to charge a small admission fee to personnel who attend our performances. Oh, nothing much! Just enough to pay costs, you understand."

A vote was promptly taken. A generous appropriation was approved at once. Permission was also granted Pume for the charging of admission with the single proviso that it must be proven by attending personnel that they were not using money owned on the purchase of Survival Certificates.

The final act of the Council was a declaration commending Priestman Pume for his imaginative and unique plan designed to insure the continued success of Cityside's Defense and Deterrence Effort.

Now, as Pume approached the Disposal Depot, the filtered air that filled his lungs felt good and the opaque plastoid dome covering Cityside seemed to him to have never been so beautiful, full as it was with the simulated fleecy clouds and the yellow balloon of the sun moving predictably in their invisible tracks through their electrical channels.

Up ahead, Pume saw one of his Priestmen approaching at the head of a long line of children, his yellow robe swirling about his black boots, his cowl shrouding the shaved dome of his head and shadowing his face. The children were singing: "The owl and the pussycat went to war in a beautiful nuclear ship." The Priestman gestured impatiently to his charges as Pume approached. Responding, they turned, each one, and made the safety sign which Pume returned with a satisfied smile. He beckoned the Priestman to his side. "Who are these children?" he asked.

"From Sector Fifteen School, sir. They are on their way to field training where they will be taught proper foraging techniques."

"Good, good. I see they have canteens. I thought—"

"The canteens are empty, sir. Hypothetical contamination of water is part of the field problem they will solve. They will learn to find water in the soil, purify it and conserve it. A pious exercise, sir, designed to strengthen their spirit under stress and help them recognize the value of fasting under fire."

"That one over there," said Pume, pointing. "A biscuit?"

The Priestman whirled on the offender with the luminous eyes whose guilt was declared for all to see by the tiny crumbs clinging to his lips. "Attention!" bellowed the Priestman.

The boy jerked erect, a tremor running through his body. "Sir?"

"Empty your pockets!"

The boy did as he had been ordered. The one remaining fragment of the forbidden biscuit fell to the cement walkway. The Priestman strode forward and crushed it into powder beneath his boot. His hand snaked out and then quickly withdrew again into the long sleeve of his robe. A red streak appeared on the boy's face where the Priestman's hand had struck and drops of blood oozed from the gash left by his ring. The Priestman turned back to Pume. "He's really not a bad boy, sir, but discipline takes time and young bodies must be tempered. It won't happen again, sir."

Pume nodded, satisfied. To the boy, he said, "Obey your Priestman. Biscuits later. It's all for your own good, you know."

Pume watched them go, the Priestman in the lead, the children marching stiffly behind him, their arms swinging smartly. Their thin voices drifted back to him: "The owl and the pussycat went to war in a beautiful nuclear ship. They took some rations and plenty of passions, enough for a war-long trip!"

When Pume arrived some minutes later, at the outer gate of the Disposal Depot, the Priestman in charge made the safety sign and admitted him immediately. The Priestman summoned a colleague to escort Pume and, when the second Priestman appeared, he said, "Morning, sir. Ya got a requisition this time or are ya just sightseein'?" Laughter, low and phlegmatic, flooded the man's throat and dissolved into a spasm of coughing.

Pume thrust the document toward the Priestman who took it from him, glanced at it and then stuffed it into his pocket.

"A requisition, huh? Say, ya don't mind my asking, whattaya do with the psychs you been hauling outa here?"

"None of your business!" Pume snapped.

"Okay, okay. Just asking is all. Just trying to be friendly." He opened the door by pressing a button on the smooth control panel embedded in the pale wall. The door slid back soundlessly. Although he had been prepared for it, the stench that flowed out almost sickened Pume. He gagged.

The Priestman was prepared. He pressed another button on the panel and a sickish, sweet smell flowed out to drown the stench of human sweat and excrement. "Ya ready, sir?"

It was like entering a zoo that has been abandoned by its keepers. It was like entering an aviary filled with angry birds. Screams split the air. Bodies churned like bubbles in a pot of boiling water. The vast room was filled with people sitting, standing, lying on the floor, talking to themselves or others, weeping, muttering words that might have been curses, whistling, shouting monotonously.

The Priestman braced himself as the unkempt human river surged toward him. He fired his sound shocker, barely aiming, but succeeding in killing two men and a girl. The psychs flowed back, ebbing and blending with the greater mass of people pressing behind them. The Priestman held his sound shocker ready and advanced slowly. Pume noted the look of glee that twisted the corners of his mouth, saw his finger feeling the trigger of his gun.

"Screw Cityside!" screamed an old man suddenly, making an obscene gesture.

A young girl laughed lightly and twirled in endless circles, her arms thrown high above her head, dancing wildly to a rhythm only she could hear.

"I've got to go, I've got to get out," whined a woman kneeling on the floor as she sorted ragged pieces of colored cloth in neat piles in front of her. "There's roses and there's peonies and *there's* chrysanthemums. Is it time to go?"

The Priestman shoved her aside as he advanced. She scurried to retrieve her piles of rags. "My *violets!*" she shrieked at him, clutching the colored rags to her withered breasts.

"Villane!" bellowed the Priestman. He gazed around the Depot. "Villane! You got yerself a visitor!"

Pume waited tensely.

Waving his sound shocker, the Priestman cleared a path through the human debris littering the great room. He turned and gestured toward the Priestman in his turret high above them. A door opened automatically in front of them. "Quick," he said to Pume. "Through here."

They entered a smaller room overflowing with psychs where water was shooting up from vents in the floor like frothy geysers. Water also streamed down from an invisible sprinkler system in the ceiling. They stood in a dry alcove and peered into the spray.

"Calms 'em down," the Priestman told Pume. "First, hot, then cold, then hot again. Keeps 'em clean for awhile too."

"Do you see him?" Pume asked. How he hated these trips! Only by keeping his mind focused on what was yet to be was he able to endure these visits. He had made four so far. This was to be his last if all went well. He could have sent someone else but someone else might have wondered why or asked uncomfortable questions. So he came himself each time.

"Hey, Villane!" No one answered the Priestman. The psychs in the room, buffeted by the streams of water, stumbled and fell, rose and fell again. The only sound in the room was the *sssssing* of the water.

"C'mon," the Priestman said, leading Pume from the room. As the door slid shut behind them, he said, "Boy, when I get my hands on that Villane, I'll—"

"You will not touch him!" Pume said sharply. "He's mine. He belongs to me. Do you understand?"

They made their way to a huge panel of tiny colored lights that flashed on the greater part of one wall, high above the reach of the psychs. Using his key, the Priestman activated the panel and spoke into the receiver. "Psych Phillip Villane, Life Labber. Give location."

Lights flickered and flashed on the panel and then formed words which flowed from right to left across the screen: *Phillip Villane. Scheduled for relocation. Located in exit terminal.*

The Priestman roared, "They can't do nothing right around here! C'mon, sir. You want your boy, you better hurry. They got him rounded up with the others to be sent out into Landsend!"

"But," exclaimed Pume, running to keep up with his escort as he raced through the crowd of psychs, "I had my requisition in the day after I knew he'd gotten psych-sick!"

"Clerical error, maybe!" the running Priestman yelled back.

They made their way out of the Depot proper and into an open yard-like enclosure which Pume had never seen before although he had known that it existed. It was crammed with psychs and Pume saw several charred bodies lying at the outer edge of the area. "They're dead aren't they?"

"Sure, we tell them over the speaks that we've vented the dome and that the heat field's out there and that they should stay put but it's no use talking to psychs. It happens every time. Some of them run into the field and fry. Maybe it's better to go that way than to fall into the hands of the Landsenders. Villane!"

"What is the meaning of this uproar?" came the cold voice of one of the Priestmen over the speaks.

"This here's Supreme Priestman Pume and he's got a requisition for the psych Villane. You got this Villane in here among the relocates by mistake!"

"Keep the field functioning," the Priestman shouted over the speaks. There was a brief silence and then a voice ordered, "Isolate psych Villane." Priestmen moved into the arena and began searching.

Pume saw them seize a man and hustle him out of the arena.

"They got him!" his escort remarked with satisfaction. "You're lucky, sir."

"He's naked!" cried Pume, indignation ringing in his voice.

The Priestman at his side shrugged. His shrug seemed to say that if Pume didn't understand that morality was at best a sometime thing in the Disposal Depot and that all the Priestmen in Cityside couldn't enforce it, then he couldn't possibly make Pume understand. "We can go now, sir. Now that they've got him."

The Priestmen deactivated the heat field and began driving the psychs out of the Depot. "Wait!" Pume muttered huskily. "I want to see." He felt fear, imagining himself doomed to such an awful fate. When the last of the psychs was finally gone, the dome was closed again and the heat field activated from the control turret.

Pume turned and followed his guide through the door. Together they entered a sterile reception room which contained only a table, a chair and the naked man Pume had seen earlier among the relocates.

Averting his eyes, Pume ordered, "Get some clothes on him!"

Obediently, Pume's companion left the room and returned moments later with a loose fitting garment of coarse gray cloth. He threw it to the prisoner who, with a smile, put it on and said, "Now that the proprieties have been observed, perhaps we should introduce ourselves. I'm Phillip Villane."

"Villane," said the Priestman, jerking a thumb in Pume's direction, "this here's Supreme Priestman Pume. You know?"

"I know," Villane said.

"Well, well, Villane," Pume said. "Don't look so distressed. I've saved you from Landsend and, with your cooperation, I'll save you from yourself."

Villane's only response was a wry grin. The grin vanished as the sound of the Priestmen's chanted litany drifted through the open door of the room. "What's that?" Villane asked.

Pume answered, "The lament for the dead and the dying."

Villane listened, appalled.

Evil they were. The law is satisfied. Vanquished are they. The law is satisfied. Death and the gnawing worm are their lot. Now is the law satisfied!

"Come, come, Villane," said Pume, noticing the expression of disgust on Villane's face. "They had no utility any longer. They sinned through sickness and their penalty is just. Mourn not for the dead or their dying but rather sing praises to the living—to their survival and sanctity."

"I should have been with them," Villane mused.

Pume wiggled a finger in front of his face. "Cityside forgives you because Cityside needs you."

An expression of alarm, rapidly replaced by one of fury mixed with a grim determination, crossed Villane's face. "I won't go back to work in the Lab. Should you see fit to force me, I will smash the microscopes and destroy the culture dishes. I will not go back. Rather than make death, I will go to meet it. Pume, you are a fool!"

Unperturbed, Pume shook his head. "No, Villane. I am no more a fool than you are although you talk like one. Be reasonable. Hear me out at least. I have saved you from the Landsenders because I—all of us—need your intelligence and your skills and even, yes, your twisted ideals that can be straightened and turned to the service of Cityside. And, Villane, remember that you have no choice."

"I choose Landsend."

"Perhaps I am wrong. You may be a fool after all. You still cannot see that *you have no choice!* Well, then I will prove it to you. Priestman!"

The Priestman stepped forward and shoved Villane ahead of him toward the door leading from the room. Pume followed. When they had reached the entrance to the main arena of the Disposal Depot, Pume beckoned to a passing Priestman. There was a whispered conference after which the Priestman removed his sound shocker from its leather holster and entered the arena. The door closed behind him.

"We can watch from over here," Pume said, indicating a small window in the wall.

Villane let himself be led to the window. "What's this all about Pume? You're wasting your time."

"Am I? We'll see. Let me tell you about my plan and the important part you will play in it, Villane." He explained, watching Villane's face carefully. When he had finished, he asked, "Can I count on your cooperation, Villane?"

"I will do nothing to perpetuate the death-in-life that is Cityside," Villane declared.

Pume sighed and turned to the window. He signaled to the waiting Priestman who raised his gun and fired. A psych fell writhing to the floor, his body a trembling ball.

"What—!" exclaimed Villane.

"Sound shock," Pume told me. "The Priestman there fired a micro-miniaturized, high-frequency sound transmitter into the body of that poor unfortunate. Once inside, its casing dissolved. It operates above audible range at more than thirty thousand cycles a second and emits a rather complicated combination of component harmonic sounds, each of definite frequency. As the body's tissues absorb this ultrasound, intense heat is generated, causing necrosis of those tissues and subsequent death from sound shock.

"So you see the dire result of your obstinacy in the face of reason, Villane. You see the result of your refusal to cooperate with me and the other Priestmen and all right-thinking citizens who are working for the salvation of Cityside. Now I ask you again, Villane. I have infinite patience and there are hundreds of psychs in there. Will you cooperate?"

"No," Villane said after a pause.

Pume gestured at the window. The Priestman beyond it fired. Another psych fell.

"In the name of all that's sane, stop it!" Villane shouted. He found himself in the untenable position of causing death when all he wished was life.

Pume calmly repeated his question.

Slowly Villane shook his head. He saw Pume's signal, delivered like a carelessly dropped handkerchief, and his brain, a battleground, blazed. He tried to turn away from the window but felt himself thrust toward it by the Priestman, his head held immobile against the cool glass. He saw the Priestman raise his gun and point it at the open-mouthed psych cringing on his knees in the middle of the arena whose screams he could not hear. "All right!" he cried, tearing himself free of the Priestman's grip. "All right. But stop it, stop it, stop it!"

Pume reached out and patted his quaking shoulders. "Sensible decision, Villane. Too bad for those psychs that it took so long to make. But sensible, however delayed."

Villane recoiled from Pume's touch as from the touch of a scorpion.

Pume signaled to the Priestman inside the arena, indicating that his services would no longer be needed. The Priestman promptly holstered his gun and left the arena.

"To insure your future and complete cooperation," Pume was saying, "let me promise you, Villane, that for every refusal you offer a psych will die of sound shock. Now we understand each other, do we not?"

Numbly, Villane nodded.

"Good. Now perhaps we can make progress. You'll find that it will not be as bad as you might imagine. On the contrary, I venture to predict that you will enjoy working with me and the others. You will like the results of your work and if you are on occasion troubled and tempted to do something foolish, why, just remember what you've seen here today. And remember too, my dear Villane, that I will not be so kind or so stupid as to have you killed. That would be too easy and, if I may say so, a pandering of the lowest sort to the darker images lurking within your own neatly catalogued categories of what you, I imagine, would call your ideals."

Villane felt beaten. Despite himself, he was once again, although unwillingly and unwittingly this time, the potential cause of someone's death, not on a mass scale this time but on an individual, personal level. He glanced back through the window at the limp and lifeless bodies and the draining blood.

Pume, watching him carefully, said, "Sound shock also splinters bones which then tear the skin and rupture vital internal organs."

Like a bewildered dog beaten for no reason it can understand, Villane shook his head wearily and, like a dog, followed the beckoning Pume from the room, thinking that Death was on the march and hiding behind every door and that he, Villane, was enlisted in its legions for as long as he should live.

As they rode up on the pneumatic tube to Pume's two hundred and fourth floor apartment, Villane was silent, listening to Pume's chatter.

"I have such plans," Pume was saying, rubbing his plump palms together. "You won't be sorry, Villane, I promise you, when you see what all of us together can accomplish for the good of Cityside, for the peace of our people. They're deserving, no question about that. Loyal, dedicated and deserving."

Villane spat an epithet which Pume ignored.

"If we're to save Cityside," he continued, growing enthusiastic, "we've got to prevent psych-sickness." He glanced covertly at Villane. "Not only the more evident forms of it but also the more insidious forms manifested in people like yourself, Villane."

Villane remained silent.

"Here we are," Pume announced as the pneumatic tube whirred to a stop and the door opened in front of them. "Welcome to my home!"

Villane gazed about him at the gigantic room in which he found himself. It was lushly furnished with formfit furniture and thick red rugs. Tasteless, Villane decided, but opulent. Befitting Cityside's Supreme Priestman. Occupying most of one wall was a deluxe serviset. Floor vents hummed and hidden light fixtures bathed the room in a rich radiance of pale pink light.

As the door slid soundlessly shut behind them, Pume threw back his cowl and went to the serviset. "What will you have, Villane?"

Villane shook his head.

"Now, now. No petulance, please. How about a caffein?"

"Diluted."

Pume dialed drinks and the serviset promptly produced the caffein and a glass filled with a green liquid. Villane accepted the caffein from Pume and absently rummaged in the pockets of the gray garment he still wore. His hands came up empty. "You have any scent smokes?"

"Of course."

Villane accepted the offered package, extracted a thin tube from it, switched it on and drew its aromatic mist into his nostrils. He flopped wearily into an enormous pastel chair and raised his cup to his lips as the chair fitted itself to the contours of his body.

"You'll be staying here with us, of course," Pume was saying as he moved about the room, straightening a picture here, fluffing a pillow there. "You'll have your own quarters and congenial companions. Women too, if you like. What are your tastes in that area?"

"You've bought my body, Pume," Villane snarled. "You've leased my mind. But surely you're not concerned about my gonadal needs!"

Pume laughed gaily. "I just want you to be completely happy. I can get you girls, you know, if and when you want them. Just say the word."

"Pimp!"

"What?"

"The word. I said the word."

"I have no anger to waste on you, Villane, so stop prattling, please." Pume crossed the room and pressed a button embedded in the wall near the door and then returned to stand, arms folded, in front of Villane. "I've called your colleagues," he said.

The long ash fell unnoticed from Villane's scent smoke. The floor vents whooshshed as they sucked it out of sight. "My colleagues?"

"Graduates of the same academy—the Disposal Depot. Hand-picked, each of them, by me."

Villane sprang from his chair as the little girl suddenly materialized in the room. She hadn't come through the door insofar as Villane could tell although he might have been mistaken on that point, he realized. He judged her to be no more than twelve years old. She stood there beside him in her short white skirt that revealed her bony knees and her faded blouse that had once been yellow. Her close-cropped hair formed a cinnamon helmet on her head.

"This is Sister," said Pume, amused at the startled expression on Villane's face. "Sister, this is Phillip Villane. Say hello."

"You from the Dump?" the girl asked.

"The Dump?" Villane repeated, not understanding her question.

"Oh, you know. The Disposal Depot," she told him, drawing out the last two words and giving them a kind of ludicrous dignity.

"Why, yes. Yes, I am."

"Me too. I teleport."

"Sister is only twelve years old," declared Pume, sipping his drink. "She is a very talented child. A pity that her parents were frightened by her talent. But they were and so they abandoned her years ago. My Priestmen found her and kept her in the Depot where they also kept her drugged constantly, more or less, because of her rather peculiar talent. Otherwise, she probably would have simply gone away! You've already noticed that Sister is not troubled by the barriers of solid matter as are those of us less fortunate—less talented—than she. She simply travels from place to place as she pleases and by that I mean through walls, locked doors and other such obstacles. Show him, Sister."

Sister vanished.

"Where—how?" stammered Villane.

"I cannot tell you how. Nor can Sister. Neither of us really know, you see. She's probably in her quarters now. *Sister!*"

She reappeared, expressionless, in front of Villane.

"I—I'm pleased to meet you, Sister," Villane said awkwardly, holding out his hand to her.

She merely stared at him. She did not touch his hand. "What can *you* do?" she asked, after several seconds had passed.

"Do? I'm afraid I don't understand."

"Sister wants to know," intoned the man who suddenly appeared to fill the open doorway, "what your special abilities are. Our host wouldn't have selected you simply at random."

Villane stared at the man, caught and held by his bright black eyes that were like shining pebbles in the landscape of his rugged face. Villane guessed that he might be forty years old. He had a curiously intent look mingled with an air of faint distraction like that of a man smelling rain on the wind and waiting for the first deep thud of thunder in the sky. His powerful body and limbs seemed about to burst free of the tight leather pants and saffron shirt he wore and Villane began to wonder how the room itself could contain him.

The man stepped forward and took Villane's still outstretched hand and shook it vigorously. His grip was strong, his flesh warm. "I'm Adam York," he said. "From the Dump. That's what we call it—the Dump. Much more descriptive, don't you think, than the admittedly more sanitary title of Disposal Depot. Well. Can't say it's nice to have you here. I mean no reflection on you personally. It's just that Pume's little menagerie—Sister and I and the rest—don't like it here. Or him. Pume, I mean. And chances are you won't, or don't, either."

"I'm Phillip Villane." It seemed strange to Villane to shake hands after all the days and nights and noons of making the absurd safety sign instead of enjoying this simple human contact. A rich sense of relief flowed through him. Psych-sick by Cityside's standards Adam York might well be. But he liked the man at once.

"You should show him Grandsir," Sister remarked, shifting her weight from one foot to the other, small hands glued to her bony hips.

"Yes, you're quite right," Pume said. "Come with me, Villane. There's someone else you should meet."

"I'll beat!" cried Sister, and vanished again.

They found her waiting for them when they arrived in the room that seemed to be erupting in a volcano of books.

Pointing to the old man who sat hunched over a desk littered with books, papers, light pens and a portable memory bank, Pume said, "This is Grandsir."

"Get out, get out!" cried Grandsir impatiently, squinting up at them. His hands quivered and his voice shook, whether with excitement or rage, Villane could not determine. "I'm reading, can't you see?" he shrilled, gesturing at the books flooding the top of his table and brushing with pale fingers at the thin strands of white hair that floated down about his wrinkled forehead like smoke. "You want to know about acrobats, Pume, then you get out of here and leave me be!"

"We're going, Grandsir," Pume said soothingly. "I just wanted you to meet the new arrival. Phillip Villane."

"You're Villane?" Grandsir inquired.

"Yes," Villane answered.

"Hello. Now, get out! All of you." He turned, dismissing them, and bent over a book, running a finger down a page. "Acquit, acre, acrid, *acrobat!* Now, let's see—"

"He's cranky but he knows zillions of things," Sister commented as they left the old man. "I like him."

"Has he met Gordon?" York asked Pume.

"I *hate* him!" Sister said.

"No," Pume replied. "But Gordon will be along. I think we should have something to eat now. Hungry, Sister?"

"I'll have hot dogs," Sister declared. "Grandier told me about them."

"He's corrupting you," Pume declared. "Tell him he'll have to program the serviset if you want hot dogs, whatever they are. For now, you'll settle for a freezfix."

Sister did settle but complained vociferously as she spooned the food into her mouth. York, Villane noticed, ate little and that little he chewed remorselessly like a determined cow with its cud.

"Sister," Pume said, when she had finished eating. "Take a tray to Grandsir." He waited several minutes, continuing to eat, and then, when she made no reply, he reached inside his robe, fumbled about for a moment and then withdrew his hand. At the same instant, Sister screamed, a piercing wail, her hands flying up to seize her head between them. Pume waited another few seconds before asking, "Enough? The tray then." Sister finally stopped screaming and stood up, tears glistening in her eyes. She went to the serviset and extracted a freezfix which she placed on a disposable tray. "Run along now," Pume said.

Villane watched, wondering. "What was the matter with her?"

York answered, "Another of Pume's little refinements. We have, each of us, a little item that is not normally a part of one's anatomy but happens to be part of ours. It is implanted by the most precise surgical procedures in our skulls and it has the curious ability to emit incredibly painful sound signals when Pume chooses to activate it with the little control panel he carries next to his heart.

Each of us responds to a specific harmonic frequency. It is very painful."

Villane swung around to stare at Pume. He found it difficult to believe that, beneath the man's seemingly mild exterior, lay a capability for cruelty and ruthlessness that Villane had never seen surpassed. But the tears in Sister's eyes had testified to the truth of this fact as had her screams. So had the corpses Villane had seen in the Disposal Depot.

"Pume is monstrous," York said simply.

"Ah, here is Gordon," cried Pume, waving his arm gaily in the direction of the dwarf who was loping with a lopsided gait across the room toward them.

Villane had at first mistaken the dwarf for a crippled child. Gordon walked like an inexperienced sailor on a ship tossed by heavy seas. His face was cherubic. His head supported a thick avalanche of bright blond curls. His smile, which he now bestowed upon Villane, was ingenuous and his eyes were merry.

Villane watched as the dwarf crawled up onto Pume's lap. As Pume fed him part of his own meal with fastidious fingers, York left the table.

"Villane, this is Gordon," Pume announced happily. "Gordon, I'd like you to meet Phillip Villane. He is one of us now so I want you to be nice to him. No experiments. No nastiness."

"Nastiness!" York exclaimed, turning swiftly, his eyes narrowing. "That creature created a heat field in my cleanroom yesterday. I nearly scalded myself! Nastiness, Pume?"

Gordon bounced, smiling, on Pume's lap.

Sister materialized in the room, a look of malevolence on her face as she told Pume, "Grandsir says he needs a book about clowns. He needs it now!" She flung the empty tray into the disposit and disappeared.

"Clowns, yes," Pume mused. "We shall most certainly require clowns, eh, Gordon?" He fondled the dwarfs head, ruffling the nest of blond snakes that was his hair.

Gordon's eyes grew wide. He leaped from Pume's lap as Pume stood up.

York leaned toward Villane. "Gordon's telepathic. Sends his thoughts right into your brain. Pume reads him loud and clear. The rest of us can hear him only if he lets us."

"Come along, Gordon," Pume said, taking the dwarf's hand. "Make yourself at home, Villane. We'll talk later, you and I."

Villane watched them leave the room, Pume ballooning along with the dwarf following, his grotesque satellite. When they were gone, he turned to York. "Strange little guy, isn't he?"

York snorted. "Strange, all right. That's one way of putting it."

"Pume got him from the Dump?"

York nodded. "Seems he killed a few citizens for no apparent reason one day before the Priestmen could subdue him. They deposited him in the Dump. Pume picked him because of his telepathic powers—and for other reasons too.

"He picked me because I was working in Reality Creation and Control before I finally went under. Sister's here because she's capable of teleportation. Grandsir because of all the knowledge he's managed to store up about the past from all those books he's always reading. What about you, Villane?"

"I was trained as a biochemist specializing at first in electronic manipulation of matter among other things too obscene to mention."

"What happened?"

"What happened?" Villane paused, sat down and gazed thoughtfully at the ceiling. "What happened? I couldn't take it any more. That's what happened. I couldn't do it anymore. I couldn't spend another day with death, fashioning it in test tubes and coaxing it out of molds and decayed matter because I realized the simple fact that it was *my* death too. Mine in the sense that in creating it part of me was dying."

"And you loved life, is that it?"

Villane looked up at York, saw the cynical smile come and go on his face. "No. I guess not, not really. But I couldn't do it anymore. I refused."

"But by refusing," York taunted him, "you automatically chose death. In Landsend. You knew that, didn't you?"

"I suppose so. I know it doesn't make sense."

"It does," York said solemnly. "A sick kind of sense. But that's only because of the way we live now and what we've become. I told you that I worked in Reality Creation and Control."

"Never heard of that outfit."

"No, you wouldn't have. Classified information. In RC & C, we worked closely with the Priestmen under Pume's direction and we created the slogans they use, developed the philosophy, for want of a better term, that they spew out to the people and invented, in short, the way Citysiders should think and feel about things—their lives, themselves, others, their world. Then we were told to launch some rather extraordinary electronic research on selected specimens. It's funny what you can do when you start playing with people's brains and sense centers and a few implants in the right places."

"Funny?"

"No. It's actually pretty awful. Or can be. Put an electrolytic pin in this lobe, properly stimulate the salivary glands and the olfactory nerves, for example, and you can pretty much create a specific, controlled reality for that specimen on a temporary basis."

"All for the good of Cityside, of course," Villane said.

"Precisely."

"You psyched-out?"

"No, I quit. Same thing. Like you, I'd had it right up to here. Then, the Dump. But Pume had other plans for me. He pulled me out of the Dump and now, thanks to this little parasite," York continued, tapping the metal disk studding his skull above his left ear, "Pume has me back at work and keeping busy."

35

"He's planning to use your—your skill in his circus?"

"He is. I've rigged up a gadget that we call the Funforall. We added a few gimmicks and a bit of window dressing, so to speak, to impress the paying public but actually it's just a mildly complex computer with simple programs that can be electronically linked to a living organism to create intensely stimulating sense patterns. You'll see soon enough."

"But why did you do it? Why did you give in to Pume?"

"Pain," York replied, "pure and simple. I can't stand the pain of sound-shock. You saw what it did to Sister. Pain," he repeated. Then, "I might ask you the same question, Villane. Why are you here? You told me how you got to the Dump and that Pume requisitioned you but why did you let him?"

Villane explained about the Priestman and the corpses. "So you see, I had no choice."

"Ah, but you did. You could have refused until the Priestman had killed every single psych. After all, they'll be sent out into Landsend to be killed anyway. No, Villane, I think my reason is more compelling than yours although we are both, in our own ways, cowards. You know, of course, that you will be given one of these?" York indicated the receiver set in his skull. "Gordon again," he explained. "He's a surgeon, quite skilled," he said, and the bitterness was like ice in his voice.

"Feeling better a bit?" Pume asked.

Villane managed to sit up and swing his legs over the edge of the table on which he had been lying. He looked around the laboratory in which he found himself and saw Gordon astride a low shelf, gazing at him and grinning.

"I must have passed out," he said. He felt dazed and disoriented. What was this room? What day was it? What had happened to him?

"No," Pume said quietly. "You were drugged so that there would be no difficulty during the operation. Gordon's finished with you now."

Gordon's thoughts nudged Villane's mind, ". . . a little pain for a little while once the drug wears off. Nothing much."

Villane raised his hand and felt the smooth metal disk set in his skull just above his left ear. He remembered York's warning. He picked at the plate with his fingers as if it were a new species of scab.

"Leave it alone, Villane!" Pume ordered.

Gordon jumped down from his perch and sidled up to Pume. Villane guessed that Pume was listening to the dwarf's unspoken words.

Pume glanced at Villane and grinned. "Gordon suggests a test. A good idea. A splendid idea. Brace yourself, Villane!" He reached beneath his robe and suddenly chaos exploded inside Villane's head.

He screamed and fell from the table. A shrill, piercing sound riddled his brain and set his bones shuddering. The walls of the room rippled and the floor fell away beneath him. A swimmer sinking in an endless sea, Villane heard his own screams blending with the ultrasound that seemed to be shattering his very skin as he struggled vainly with his unseen enemy.

As suddenly as it had begun, it stopped. Silence fell like a soft blanket on Villane where he lay sobbing on hands and knees on the cold floor. He struggled to stand up but his quaking legs betrayed him and he slumped like a dropped doll to the floor at Pume's feet. He raised one hand to his face and felt shame as he touched the wetness leaking from his eyes. But the pain had been worse than anything he had ever known or imagined. Humiliation shrouded him and he forced himself to rememder that he was a man and that he must stand up, stand up and not let himself be so badly broken.

Gordon, like a gadfly, hopped about him, waving his arms and clapping his hands.

Villane finally managed to get to his feet. As he leaned against the table for support, he avoided looking at Pume, his tormentor. But Pume, as if knowing his thoughts, stepped forward and said, "Look at me, Villane!"

Villane obeyed. He felt rage. Then shame. Shame because he knew the uselessness of his rage. He knew his own helplessness and the bondage he shared now with the others—with Grandsir and Sister, York and— He suddenly realized that Gordon wore no metal plate in his head.

"Let me warn you, Villane," Pume told him in a steady voice. "It is quite useless to think of attacking me. Before you could take two steps toward me, I would press one button, yours, and you would be whimpering on your knees before me like an animal biting its own wounds in a desperate attempt to end its pain. Our contract is signed and sealed. We are bound together, you and I. If it troubles you, this thought, erase it from your mind. Just cooperate with me and the others and you need never again be reminded of what has happened here this morning. You will be able to think of yourself as your own man and forget that you are not, that you are *mine!*"

"I'll kill you, Pume!" Villane heard himself mutter.

Pume chuckled, his chins jiggling on his chest. "I doubt it, although each of the others have tried. Even Grandsir, the feeble old fool. And you will too in time, I suppose, despite my warning. But then you'll learn the futility of such action. You'll soon discover that you will want to help me and court my pleasure and you'll learn to pretend that you do it for reasons you have not yet rationalized into existence because the alternative for you is—' Pume left the sentence unfinished and let his hand glide like a serpent toward his chest.

"No!" cried Villane. "Please." Instantly, he was overwhelmed again with despair and shame. He knew that Pume was right. His own tortured plea had proved that rightness.

Pume let his hand drop. "Well, that's that then." Turning to Gordon, he said, "Give our friend something for the pain. We have work to do."

Gordon scurried to a cabinet standing against the wall, hopped up on a stool, opened the door of the cabinet and withdrew a small bottle filled with purple capsules. He extracted one and returned to stand in front of Villane, his hand held up, the purple capsule resting in his small palm. Villane took the capsule and promptly swallowed it.

"One or two more points, Villane," Pume said. "Obviously, it will not be necessary for me to return to the Depot and arrange for the liquidation of a few more psychs to insure your cooperation. That was enough to get you out of there but such a crude method is no longer needed. And don't think of killing yourself. Such an act would not mean escape, not really, because we would only revivify you and you would not like that, I can assure you. Which brings me to the matter at hand. Come along, please. I have something to show you."

Villane followed Pume from the room, leaving Gordon alone in the laboratory. They entered another room which Villane had never seen during the three days he had been in Pume's apartment. The walls of the room were lined with glass upon which grew a thin frost like a white moss.

"Your workshop, Villane," Pume announced, with a theatrical wave of his hand.

Villane looked around him at the steel tables, the instruments, the forked fingers of light flashing between the two globes high above what Villane immediately recognized as a matter manipulator. He had come full circle, he realized with a sense of profound shock.

"The creation of toxins or viral cultures will not be required of you here, Villane," Pume said. "I have something else in mind. I know that you've worked on matter manipulation with Kleitmann and were considered his prize pupil. I know that you did some of your best work during Kleitmann's life loan experiments. Now you will have the opportunity of continuing that work but for a slightly different purpose."

"I don't understand."

"Let me explain." Pume went to the glass wall and beckoned to Villane. When they stood side by side, Pume gestured at the transparent wall. Villane cupped his hands to his face and peered through the frosted glass. Inside, bathed in a sickly yellow light, lay bodies of all sizes and ages and both sexes. Villane guessed that there were at least a score of them. He turned a questioning gaze on Pume.

"Our circus," Pume said, "Grandsir has discovered from his research, will require what our ancestors used to call freaks. But, as you know, our eugenics program has virtually eliminated such creatures from our society. Oh, on occasion, there's a rare radioactive accident or a genetic failure that goes undetected and a Gordon or a Sister is born. The point is, however, that for our circus we need freaks and you, Villane, will create them for us!"

"How?" Villane asked, but he guessed that he already knew.

"Matter manipulation," Pume replied. "These corpses are from the Depot. You will revivify them and, uh, change them a bit. They'll be one of our star attractions, thanks to your very special skills."

Villane felt horror, like a great evil bird, swoop down on him. It perched, like a witch's familiar, on his shoulder and he told himself that he would have to get used to it, awful though it was.

"The first thing you must do, Villane, is consult with Grandsir who has found pictures of freaks in one of his books. I've thought about this for some time and I suggest that you let your imagination soar. I want no mere fat ladies or giants. What I require is something a bit more imaginative. Something that will send our patrons away marveling. Now, get busy."

When Pume had gone, Villane strode about the laboratory, checking instruments and examining dials and gauges.

Grandsir appeared suddenly in the doorway. "Here it is," he said, holding out a black book with gold stamping on its spine. "The book says there were always freaks in circuses." He opened the book and flipped through its pages. "Here they are. See."

Villane took the book in his hands and looked at the colorful photographs. There were two tiny people with pointed heads pictured on one page. There was a man with no arms and no legs, only a head and a torso, staring vacantly at nothing and men whose tattooed skin was a picture book in itself.

"You look all done in, boy," Grandsir observed, studying Villane. "Something bad happen to you?"

"Yes," Villane answered, "something very bad."

"Sorry for you, boy. Sorry for all of us. Wish he'd let us go to Landsend. Better that than this. How old are you, boy?"

"Twenty-seven."

"I'm one hundred and fourteen thanks to the success of the science of geriatrics and I'm tired, tired of it all. Even the books make me tired now. I had a bookstore once before Earth War Three."

"A bookstore?"

"That was a place where there were lots and lots of books and people came in to look at them, maybe buy them and take them home and read them. It was different back then. No tapes or filmfax machines or stuff. People *read* then, boy!"

The thought of people reading was strange to Villane who had grown up in the study cribs and with the filmfax. "Where'd you get this book, Grandsir?"

"Pume gets lots of them for me. The Priestmen have most of them locked away tight someplace so they don't make people nervous or anything. You'd be surprised at the things that there are in some of those books. Oh, I'll say!"

Villane turned the pages and read the captions under the colorful photographs. At last he put the book down and stood up slowly. He went to the wall and studied the control panel for several minutes and then turned several dials, following printed directions on the panel. Behind the wall, the corpses rotated on their slabs like parts of a circular conveyor belt. Villane chose one. He flicked a switch and the rotatory movement stopped. He opened the glass panel in the wall and withdrew the slab which held the body of what had once been a young man. Deftly, he slid the table under it and removed the body. He wheeled it under the blinding lights and left it momentarily, turning to lace himself into the sterile gown he found hanging beside the wash basin, scrub his hands and draw on the rubber gloves that had been resting as if waiting on the basin shelf. He returned to the table, adjusted his mask and focused the scanner of the matter manipulator on the shoulders and arms of the pale corpse. He switched the machine on, adjusted the intensity indicators and set the flux schedule. The corpse seemed to shift position slightly as the rays streamed down upon it like colored rain. Its arms slowly shriveled and transmuted, leaving a faint trace of fine gray ash on the table. Villane waited, counting the seconds, watching the ash reform itself, seeing the corpse begin to change.

At last, when it was over, Grandsir marveled, "Why, he's full of ginger, isn't he? Look at him sit up there so sprightly!"

Villane sighed.

The young man slid off the table and moved jerkily about the room in response to the electrical implants stimulating his muscles. *"Aaggh,"* he moaned, his eyelids flickering independently of each other, fluttering the great feathery wings that now sprouted from his shoulders, searching with vacant eyes for the arms he vaguely remembered once owning.

"You ought to be ashamed, boy," Grandsir commented wearily. "We all of us ought to be ashamed."

"Why, you've done marvelously, Villane!" Pume crowed, fairly vibrating with pleasure as he walked about the laboratory examining the results of Villane's effort. "And in less than a week!"

Villane said nothing.

"This one is superb!" Pume exulted. "Wings, no less! I have to congratulate you, Villane, on your vivid imagination."

"Rabid imagination, I'd call it," Villane murmured too softly for Pume to hear. He helped the winged figure to his feet so that Pume could get a better look. The creature stood, eyes glazed, staring beyond the walls of the room into nowhere, somewhere. Its muscles jerked and shuddered as electrical impulses stirred its revivified body. Its wings fluttered feebly.

"Magnificent!" Pume declared, rubbing his hands together and moving on down the line of revives. "This one —wonderful!"

"This one" had been an elderly woman. Faint traces of her humanity remained and hints of her femininity could still be discerned in the curved outlines of her now distorted form. She was covered with fur, blue, and stooped, not with age, but with the weight of the two huge mounds of flesh that hung from her thin arms in place of hands. As Pume prodded her with his foot, she mewled and looked up at him with one of her three eyes.

"They're drugged," Villane commented. "It keeps them passive but there's a problem."

"Problem? What do you mean?" Pume sputtered.

"Care," Villane replied. "They need looking after. They need someone to administer their electroid rations and clean up after them. As you can see, they slobber, some of them, and—well, worse."

"Yes," Pume said, pondering.

"Perhaps Gordon could—"

"No!" Pume stated flatly. "Gordon can't be allowed to —what I mean is, he's busy with other things."

"Why don't you tell the truth, Pume? What you mean is that Gordon might want to experiment with these revives, isn't it?"

Pume gave Villane a noncommittal smile. "Forget Gordon. But you're right—we must have a caretaker for these freaks."

The sudden sound startled them. Like the squeal of a pig in a slaughterhouse that feels the knife at its throat, the cry went up from the winged freak, gluing Villane and Pume to the floor where they stood, as the fat tears welled up and slipped free of the creature's eyes to roll down its cheeks and fall, with no sound, on its scrawny chest.

Villane went to the creature, gently forcing it to sit down again on the floor as he wiped its face with a piece of gauze he had found in his pocket. He patted its shoulder and the cries subsided until the only sound in the room was the mewling of the blue-furred woman as she scratched herself where the saliva slipping from her lips had fallen on and crusted her fur.

"Interesting reaction," Pume mused. "One seldom sees such an obvious emotional reaction in revives."

Villane turned to face Pume. He ground his teeth together and then made a conscious effort to relax before he spoke. "What are you going to do about caring for these people, Pume?"

Pume was still studying them but the word Villane had used caught his fancy and he said, *"People,* Villane? *Revives!* That's your trouble, you know. You let yourself get upset over nothing. You have a job to do, you're doing it and doing it well, and that's all you need care about. These *things* are not people. They are *revives!* Try to remember that. You'll feel better. Now, the problem."

Pume picked up the visifone and spoke the code numerals for the Disposal Depot as Villane tried to quiet the blood that was burning through his body's canals. "I want to enter a requisition for one of your personnel," Pume told the Priestman whose face flashed on the dimensional screen of the visifone.

"Excuse me, sir," said the Priestman, "but nearly all of our personnel have been relocated. The Depot is empty except for the few personnel admitted this morning."

Pume ignored him. "I will give you the qualifications of the type I need. You will record them and make out the requisition. You will then forward it through channels while I wait here and you will inform me at once if there is a person there who fills these qualifications."

The chastened Priestman nodded and picked up a light

pen and waited for Pume to continue. As Pume spoke, he recorded the data Pume gave him on his computape and waited for the results. When they came, he read, "Female. Age twenty-five. Formerly employed in Life Laboratory, Project Death Development. Transferred to Nursery Science. Suffered psych-sickness. Scheduled for immediate relocation."

"Hold her in the Depot," Pume ordered. "I'll pick her up this afternoon."

When Pume had replaced the visifone, Villane asked, "Couldn't you hire someone? A Priestman, maybe?"

"Everyone else, as you should know, has his appointed job to perform," Pume snapped. "It is only the psychs who are available for projects such as ours. Does it distress you to think I am going to save someone from Landsend?"

"I suppose it's better to be here than in Landsend."

"Certainly it is! For a scientist—a supposedly objective and rational man—you amaze me, Villane. You think with your viscera!"

Villane winced and swallowed the rebuke in silence as Pume made for the door. "I'll be back shortly," he said, "and I'll have your caretaker with me. As the Priestmen say, where there's a will there's a way." The door slid shut behind him and Villane sat down on a stool, his hand rising unbidden to worry the metal disk on his skull, the badge of his bondage to Pume.

Pume identified himself to the Priestman at the gate of the Disposal Depot. He explained that he had entered a requisition that morning and asked if his psych were ready to depart. The Priestman summoned a colleague who greeted Pume familiarly, "Back again, hey? Who's it this time, sir?"

Stonily, Pume told him, "I will wait in the reception area. Get the requisition from your superiors. Bring the girl to me there."

The Priestman frowned but obeyed. Pume entered the Depot and headed for the reception room. Once inside, he sat down to wait. Less than five minutes passed before the door opened and the Priestman Pume had dispatched returned, his hand on the arm of the girl he was leading. Pume looked up and experienced a flash of recognition. He had seen this girl somewhere before. He tried to recall the time and place. Just who was she? Where had he seen her?

She was thin as birch trees are thin and strands of the uncombed cloud of her straight black hair touched her shoulders. Her breasts were small but rounded, like ripening fruit. Her slender hands hung at her sides and her sad eyes beneath the threads of her eyebrows studied Pume warily.

"Come here, girl," Pume said.

She took a tentative step toward him.

"Closer."

She advanced until she stood less than a foot away from him.

"Do you know me, girl?"

She nodded slowly. "You are Supreme Priestman Pume," she said, her tone listless.

"Then we've met before?"

"On the street about two weeks ago. You questioned me. I was crying. I denied it."

As recollection came to Pume, he smiled benignly. "Ah, yes. The girl with the tears in her eyes who insisted it was the wind, only the wind. Then it wasn't?"

She shook her head and repeated, "I was crying."

"A small world, Cityside," Pume observed. "They've told you that you're to come with me?"

"Yes."

Pume was pleased. The girl seemed manageable. Perhaps, he speculated, a sound receiver would not be needed in her case. But, he told himself, it would be safer if she had one and Gordon would be sorely disappointed if he were denied the opportunity to work on this pretty little thing. "Come along then. Oh, your name?"

"Ruth Cameron."

"Yes, I remember now. You told me that morning

when we first met." He gestured and she walked through the door like an automaton, Pume following, admiring the see-saw sway of her hips.

The Priestman at the gate winked at Pume and rolled his slitted eyes which seemed to say that Pume and he shared a good joke. Pume did not return the wink and the sternness of his expression momentarily dismayed the Priestman who took refuge in bluster. "Do you require an escort, sir? Is the girl dangerous? I'll be glad to call a—"

Pume silenced him with a glare. He led Ruth to the nearby carveyor which they boarded. They sat together, side by side, as the carveyor belt moved forward, gathering momentum.

Ruth stared straight ahead, her hands resting idly, palms up, in her lap. "Do you ever wonder," she said, addressing Pume without looking in his direction, "what would happen if someone took a little pin and pushed it into the dome covering Cityside?"

The question startled Pume. He quickly reminded himself that it was virtually impossible to tell what psychs would say—or do. He glanced covertly at Ruth. She seemed placid enough. Her face was calm and her words, although alarming in content, were spoken quietly. "No," Pume said, "I have never wondered about such things. And you shouldn't either. It isn't healthy."

"If someone did," Ruth went on, "the sky would fall, wouldn't it? The sun would plop down and the stars would die and Landsenders would pour through the little hole like mice and gobble up Cityside as if it were one big, tasty cheese."

"You're upset," Pume said uneasily. It was all he could think of to say.

"No, I'm not." She looked up at the mechanical arch of the blue sky above them with its ever present sun and white clouds. "Just for once," she whispered, "I'd like to see the sun."

"Well, look then!" Pume said, feeling anger rise red within him at her foolishness.

She gave a little laugh that had no joy in it. "No, I

mean the *real* sun I imagine must be up there somewhere. Do you suppose there really is one? Up there, beyond that silly balloon that's pretending to be the sky. And at night, stars that machines can't turn on and off like a datafix or factclock."

Pume had no time to answer. The warning *beep-ba-beep-ba-BEEP* droned through the streets like a giant insect and the carveyor ground to a halt. People rose and disembarked, positioning themselves against the buildings, pressing their backs against the granite and glass, their hands folded devoutly in front of them, their eyes lowered, their voices raised in the rising, falling, monotonous hum that signaled the beginning of another Allegiance Alert.

Steadily, the podiums on which the Priestmen stood extended themselves upward like steel flowers unfolding until the Priestmen astride them towered above the heads of the citizens humming hypnotically far below. From beyond the heat field, through the suddenly vented sections of the dome, came the weird whine as the released rockets rose up and headed toward Landsend. There came the *splat* as the biobombs were launched, carrying in their metal wombs invisible but deadly bacilli.

Pume flattened himself against the side of the nearest building. Seconds later, he realized that Ruth was not beside him. He spotted her standing alone beside the stalled carveyor. He leaped from his place under the watchful eyes of the Priestmen who saw everything and forgave nothing. He seized Ruth and dragged her back toward the nearest building. He turned her around and pressed her, with sweating hands, into place beside him.

Beep-ba-beep-ba-BEEEEPPP!

He raised his voice to join the others in the ceremony of the Allegiance Alert:

"Save Cityside, save! Save Cityside! Save, save, save!"

The Priestmen threw back their cowls and raised their arms. "They hear Evil! They see Evil! They speak Evil! Such is the way of our enemy. Truth does not walk among them nor does honor prevail in the hearts of their children. Evil they are and evil forever!"

The people moaned and their cry slithered out into the streets like a loathsome night thing, covered with the dripping slime of hate: *"Evil forever and ever!"*

"Speak the unspeakable!" cried the Priestmen from their perches.

"Landsend!" responded the people.

"Who will save us?" implored the Priestmen.

A woman ran out into the street and screamed to the Priestmen above her, her hands raised in supplication, her eyes rolling, "Me, me, me!"

"Will you save us and Cityside?"

"Yes! Yes!"

"How will you save us and Cityside?"

"I will work hard. Work wins. I *will!*" The woman quivered in the sudden condemning silence. Seconds passed. The Priestmen at last declared, "Twenty-two per cent. Below the norm. Not enough. Not nearly!"

The woman cried out in desperation, fingers tearing through her hair, "I will name you names! I name Josh Haverlind. He was *singing* in the Life Lab and he *spilled* cancer cells. I name—!"

"Twenty-two per cent," the Priestmen, relentless, intoned.

The woman, chastised, crept back to cry alone against the side of a building.

"Landsend lives!" bellowed the Priestmen in unison.

A man whirled away from his place, spittle flying, as he shouted beseechingly to the Priestmen, "Roll back the dome! Deactivate the heat field! Invade Landsend now!"

He was quickly joined by others, their arms flailing each other, their feet kicking each other in a passionate frenzy, screaming what might have been words.

Pume felt the blood beating in his head and the sweat blossom on his brow as he avidly watched the orgy of anger rage in the clean streets.

"Allegiance!" shouted the Priestmen. "Allegiance is alpha and omega!"

Pume exulted in a sweaty exuberance as the whine of the rockets died away and the distant sound of the dropping biobombs faded and the Allegiance Alert came to an end.

In his excitement, he failed to notice that Ruth had moved away from his side and stepped out into the middle of the mob that was tearing at its collective flesh like some self-destructive organism. He ran to her but he was too late to stifle the shout that erupted from her throat like a geyser.

"Seize her!" screamed the Priestmen.

The mob, to a man, froze. Like sleepwalkers startled awake, they looked about them as they sought the source of the shout. Fastening their angry eyes upon Ruth, they advanced toward her. Once more she opened her mouth and again she cried out to them, begging them to stop their battling as the Priestmen continued calling for her apprehension and arrest.

Pume reached her in time. "Stand back!" he bellowed, and the mob obeyed. Raising his eyes to the Priestmen now descending on their shrinking pillars, he declared, "I am Pume, your Supreme Priestman. This girl is in my charge. She is psych-sick."

The Priestmen immediately instructed the crowd to ignore the psych lest pollution filter out to them from her. They raised their cowls about their heads and stepped down from their pillars and moved solemnly among the throng, spraying antiseptic on bruises and wounds, injecting adrenalin antidote into the bodies of the still violent and enthusiastically selling Survival Certificates to eager buyers.

Pume led the dazed Ruth away as the blinding sun flashed in the dome overhead. He took her arm and helped her back aboard the carveyor as streams of frothy water spewed out from hidden hoses to wash away the blood and bits of torn clothing littering the area.

The Priestmen resumed their normal duties of controlling the carveyors and directing the aeroautos through the once again busy streets and calling out to their brethren, "All's swell that works well. Keep smiling!"

"You could have been killed!" Pume raged in Ruth's ear. "You could have gotten us both killed, you little idiot!"

"I meant no harm," she sighed.

"Well, you can thank my quick thinking for your present safety. You saw the faces of that mob? They would have ripped you to pieces."

Ruth said nothing. She glanced up at the orange eye of the sun overhead and grimaced.

Some time later, as they disembarked from the carveyor, Ruth followed Pume into the building and entered the pneumatic tube that would lift them to his apartment. As it shot upward, her stomach lurched and her mouth went dry. It was not fear she was experiencing so much as a complete absence of feeling, of caring. She found herself suspended between a past she abhorred and a future she could not fathom. In a state of dismal numbness, she felt herself drifting, uncertain of who she was or why she was. She stared dumbly back at the image of the girl reflected in the smooth metal walls of the tube who looked so familiar but who was, after all, a stranger.

As they entered Pume's apartment, Gordon greeted them, dancing about Pume's legs and throwing his thoughts about like darts. *"She's not bad. What are we going to do with her? Can I—?"*

Ruth, although she could not hear Gordon's thoughts, felt a surge of anxiety as he whirled about her, eating her with his eyes.

"Sit down, Ruth," Pume said. It was an order. And another, "Gordon, stay away from her!"

"You know, Ruth," Pume went on, "that Cityside is engaged in a mighty effort to prevent a recurrence of Earth War Three. You contributed to that effort until your illness. Too many citizens are falling prey to psychsickness and I have conceived a plan to remedy this malaise."

Ruth listened as he talked, interested despite herself.

Pume explained his plan for entertaining the citizens of Cityside with circuses in an effort to counteract the strain that resulted from the nature of the daily life of Cityside. Growing enthusiastic, he told her of what he called the brilliance of the idea, of the patriotism of his plan, and of the benefits that were bound to accrue from it.

It sounded reasonable to Ruth. She began to wonder if Pume were as awful as she had heard rumored during the free-time sessions in the Life Laboratory. Not much had been said during those times, just enough to awaken wonder in her. But the comments and the rumors had always been either incomplete or too vague and insubstantial. This, because of the fact that the Priestmen were seldom far away and sedition, in Cityside, had become equated with psych-sickness.

"And so you see, my dear Ruth, it is a worthy cause we are all engaged in and you, I feel certain, will be proud to help us. Think of it as an opportunity to regain your health and a second chance to be of service to Cityside."

"I'm not quite sure I understand. I've never heard of circuses until now and it's all rather confusing. What am I to do?"

"You will take care of some of the circus personnel. See to it that they're fed, quartered, kept clean—that sort of thing. An important task, I assure you. And, of course, you've had some experience with this sort of thing. You were, I believe, in Nursery Science?"

"Yes."

"A vital occupation these days."

A ghost of anguish fled across Ruth's face as she exclaimed, "Such things shouldn't be necessary! Have you ever been to the Nursery?" Before Pume had a chance to reply, she hurried on, her words tumbling over one another as she talked about the Nursery. "The heat field should be enough to protect us. They shouldn't have to create those—those *things!* Day after day, I saw the meditechs experiment with the breedettes. I saw them take those girls and treat them no better than experimental *an-*

imals! Do you know how the Limbos are created?" she asked Pume, referring to the subhuman creatures that patrolled the area known to the citizens as Limboland that lay just beyond the heat field surrounding Cityside.

"No," Pume lied. Actually, he knew all about the Nursery and the Limbos. Gordon had been a Nursery meditech before his murderous rampage that had caused him to be sent to the Disposal Depot and he never tired of thinking about the Nursery and Pume had listened, time and time again, with a certain savage interest, to his thoughts.

"They take the breedettes—the girls," Ruth continued in a cold tone, "and they use radium and isotopes and X-rays and instruments and they *treat*—that's their very fancy word—the foetuses the girls are bearing. When they are born, these—these *children*—"

"My dear," Pume put in, interrupting because he sensed the rising note of hysteria in Ruth's voice.

"They are *different*' Ruth said after a moment, ignoring the interruption. "Monstrous. Most of them are morons or worse. All of them are taught how to kill. None of them are human anymore!"

"Once I heard a very old and very wise Priestman say," Pume commented, "that man moves in mysterious ways his wonders to perform. I never forgot that. It's so true."

Ruth, still ignoring him, went on, "I couldn't stand the sight of the Limbos and I felt guilty about it. It wasn't their fault. They were victims of our own terror that bites at our blood and bones, night and day. But I just couldn't stand the sight of them. And I couldn't teach them. I couldn't play with them and their toys—their knives and their splinter bombs and all the rest."

"Well," Pume soothed, "that's all over now. Let me take you to your quarters where you can freshen up and then we'll meet the others."

Ruth rose and followed him, suddenly aware of the weariness that weighed on her and feeling an almost forgotten feminine urge to make herself, if not attractive, at least presentable.

Gordon watched her go, his eyes on her long black hair, as he mentally drew it back and shaved and sterilized a spot of skin above her left ear and inserted the sound receiver, connecting its tiny tentacles to the neurons of her central nervous system.

Later, when she returned to the main room, Pume was alone and waiting for her. His gaze romped over her body as he catalogued the elements of her simple beauty. He forced himself to think of practical matters. "Now we can visit your charges. This way, please."

He took her to the laboratory and, as she entered, she did not at first see the revives sprawled in their drugged stupor on the floor beyond the complicated apparatus of the matter manipulator.

Villane heard the door open and came out from the small antechamber where he had been preparing doses of narcolyte for the revives. His entry into the laboratory coincided with Ruth's gasp as she discovered the revives. Her hands flew up to cover the cavern of her open mouth and her eyes grew wide with shock.

"Get hold of yourself, girl!" Villane barked. Why was it, he wondered then, that he should find it necessary to shout at this girl unless her evident shock at sight of the revives heightened his own deeply rooted sense of guilt for having created them.

His words slashed into Ruth's consciousness as she felt herself sinking into horror.

Pume spoke quickly before Villane could say anything more or Ruth do anything foolish. "They are revives," he said. "Once they were truly alive. Now they are revivified and sedated. They are to be one of the attractions in our circus. It will all be explained to you later. For now, just remember that we call them freaks."

Ruth, who had never heard the word before, stared at Pume without comprehension. "Are these the ones you expect me to care for? The ones you referred to before as circus personnel?"

Pume nodded. "I told you that your experience in Nursery Science would be helpful to you here."

Ruth moaned and buried her face in her hands.

"You were in Nursery Science?" Villane asked her, beginning to understand Ruth's reaction. He had seen the Limbos that were the product of the Nursery. He felt sorrow begin to strangle him, a biting sorrow for the girl standing so stricken across from him.

"This is Phillip Villane," Pume said. "Villane, Ruth Cameron. She will help you solve the problem we discussed this morning."

Without understanding fully what Pume referred to, Ruth said, "I won't."

Pume, who had been expecting this, smiled. "You will! I'll leave it to Villane to explain to you that simple fact of your new life. Villane." A slight bow and Pume was gone.

Villane approached Ruth and took her hand. He led her to a metal stool and indicated to her that she should sit down. "Are you from the Dump?" he asked her. He had no sooner spoken the words than he realized he had echoed sister's words that had been addressed to him when he had arrived here a little more than a week ago. How easily, he thought, one becomes accustomed to the conditions and situations of one's life. Remembering his own lack of understanding of Sister's question, he hastily explained, "We—myelf and the others here—call the Disposal Depot the Dump."

"I was there," Ruth said in a small voice.

"So were we all." Villane set about explaining carefully, as if to a troubled child, what had only recently been explained to him by Sister, York and Grandsir. He finished and waited for the inevitable question. It came.

"But why do you do it? I can't understand why. *I* won't!"

Ruth didn't believe Villane when he explained about sound shock. Even when he showed her the metal disk in his skull and explained its purpose, she obviously thought he was lying. He did not labor the point, reasoning that the probability was great that she would soon enough learn the truth of what he said. The thought was not a pleasant one and he tried to dismiss it from his mind.

"I need your help, Ruth," he said to her.

She looked at him with clear but suspicious eyes.

"Pume has explained to me," he continued, "that in the twentieth century there were circuses and—"

"Yes, I know. He told me too."

"In the circuses there was usually a smaller show within the larger one. It was in this show that they displayed what they called freaks. These freaks were often victims of glandular disorders or birth accidents and they had chosen to display themselves for profit. We have almost no such types today as you know and so Pume conceived the idea of revivifying some of the dead and altering their physical structure somewhat so that his circus might have its quota of freaks."

"You did that?" Ruth asked, pointing to the revives on the floor.

Steeling himself, Villane answered, "I did."

Ruth could find no words to express the loathing she felt for Villane. Her expression indicted him and it was only with great effort that he could restrain himself from striking this silly girl who condemned without comprehension and who accused without understanding. He wondered what she would be like when Gordon was finished with her.

"I did," he repeated. "One does what one must do," he added, knowing she could not possibly understand. Not yet.

Ruth stood up and walked slowly across the room to stand staring down at the revives. Villane could not see her face but he could hear the sounds that ripped from her throat and he saw her shoulders shake.

"It's no use crying," he told her harshly. "Get busy and feed them!"

Slowly, she turned until she was facing him again. "You are less than a man, Villane!" Then, firmly, "I'm getting out of here!"

"You can't!" he exclaimed, wishing she could.

Her lips twisted in a sneer that stole all the beauty from her face. "Watch me," she said.

As she threw open the door, Villane tried to seize her arm. She struck him across the face and strode resolutely down the hall. Gordon materialized suddenly from nowhere, guarding the door that led to the pneumatic tube. His thoughts fondled Ruth's mind. *"Going somewhere?"* She halted, looking around her for the source of the question.

Guessing what had happened, Villane said, "Gordon's telepathic."

Ruth tried to push Gordon aside. It was like trying to move a boulder. His strength was inversely proportional to his size. He actually seemed to be enjoying Ruth's clumsy mauling. But at last it was apparent that he had had enough. He raised a small foot and viciously kicked Ruth's leg. She howled with pain and fury flashed in her eyes. She flung a contemptuous glance at Villane who stood with his hands at his sides. Her glance seemed to say that if he could not help her she would do what must be done herself. She reached out to grab Gordon but he slipped from her grasp like a slick salmon. As she reached for him again, Gordon's hypodermic needle gleamed like a silver firefly and bit into the flesh of Ruth's upper arm. Villane stood helplessly by as surprise flooded her face and she drifted slowly to the floor like a leaf falling from a tree frozen by winter's icy breath.

Gordon thought at Villane. *"Neat?"*

Villane turned swiftly and walked out of the room. Ruth's words nipped at his heels as he headed back to the laboratory, *"You are less than a man!"* She is right, he thought, shivering in the warm room.

That evening, Sister burst into the room like a rocket. "Who's she?" she asked, pointing at Ruth who sat slumped in a chair in the corner.

"Ruth Cameron," York answered, as he flipped the pages of one of Grandsir's books. "Gordon's got to her as you can see."

Villane entered the room. He avoided looking at Ruth.

An unspoken bond seemed to exist between them now, woven of a mutual embarrassment of which they were the singular polarities.

"You from the Dump?" Sister asked.

They all waited, watching Ruth, pitying her.

She nodded.

Sister went to the serviset and dialed an apple. Extracting it, she bit into it and, with her cheeks bulging, commented, "Thought so."

"Ruth," Villane ventured, "this is Sister. Over there, Adam York. Grandsir, you'll meet. Gordon you know."

Ruth said softly, "I'm sorry, Villane."

He brushed the apology aside.

"Sorry for what?" Pume asked, as he came into the room with Grandsir behind him.

"For judging," Ruth replied.

"Nice to have someone pretty for a change," Grandsir declared, approaching Ruth and bowing with exaggerated courtliness. "Pleased to meet you."

Ruth gave him her hand which he kissed lightly.

York said, "This is Grandsir, Ruth. Centenarian, book bug, and catalyst of our little group."

"Oh, shut up!" Sister exclaimed, thinking York had insulted Grandsir.

York's eyebrows shot up to form croquet hoops over the black balls of his eyes and his face assumed an expression of mock chagrin. "Such noise from such little lungs!"

"Villane," Pume prompted, "your laboratory. Haven't you things to do there? Ruth?"

They understood. Together, they left the room as Sister worried her apple with her small teeth and York yawned.

When they were alone in the laboratory, an uneasy silence settled on them. Villane fought for words. Finally, not looking directly at Ruth, he said, "Was it—?"

"Awful," she responded.

It was enough. At last they were able to meet each other's eyes.

"They must be hungry," Ruth said, indicating the revives.

Villane switched on the laboratory's serviset and when the food was ready, placed it on the lab table. Ruth took a bowl of steaming gruel and, kneeling down before the revives, began spooning it into their limp mouths.

The whimpering and mewling grew louder as the revives fed. They reached out with taloned claws and thick paws to clutch at Ruth and at the bowl in her hand. At first, she drew back shuddering but then, making a strong effort to overcome her distaste, she bent down and continued her task, murmuring soft and soothing sounds until each creature had eaten.

She placed the empty bowl back on the table and sighed. "They're like us," she said softly.

"What do you mean?" Villane asked.

"Not dead. Not alive. Like us."

A scream tore into the laboratory. Ruth jumped and Villane ran to the door. They raced into the living room where they found Pume, his hand hidden beneath his coat, and Sister, screaming.

"Now!" Pume snarled.

Sister remained motionless, what was left of her apple clutched in her rigid fingers.

"Now!" Pume shouted, furious. "Dance!"

He pressed Sister's button on his transmitter and she screamed again. And began to dance. Dropping her apple, she twirled this way and that, her arms thrown out, sobs and screams her accompaniment.

Pume, addressing Villane and Ruth, said, "We're rehearsing for the circus. Our little actress here has been displaying her artistic temperament. But we'll soon cure her of that. Oh, won't we just!"

Sister twirled. Pume waved his free hand as if conducting.

Ruth turned her face to the wall. Villane closed his eyes.

"Ah, tum taddy *tum!*" Pume murmured. "Now, turn left. Now, right. Splendid. Splendid!"

59

PART TWO

The Festival

"STOP YER PUSHIN'!" snarled the man as he waited in the long line outside Cityside's visitorium with the hundreds of others who had come to see Pume's circus.

"You think we'll get seats?" the woman with him asked. "I mean if there's not enough seats so we might as well go home is all."

People talking.

"—feet hurt."

"Lissen, guy, quit yer pushin' or I'll—!"

Music coaxing with rhythmic voices. Colored lights flashing into life, dying, being born again. Posters with foot-high words testifying to the wonders waiting inside the visitorium:

SEE SISTER! CHAINS CANNOT CONFINE HER. MATTER MELTS BEFORE HER. SEE SISTER!

"I'm getting awful tired of waiting, Lars. Let's—"

GET YOUR TICKETS. WIN A TRIP IN THE FUNFORALL!

Metallic music.

SEE THE FREAKS!

"What's freaks anyhow?"

Shrugged shoulders.

FEATURING THE GLORIOUS GORDON—THE PRINCE OF PAIN.

At last the ticket seller. Plastoid coins change hands. Tickets are dispensed. "Pass, please. Next, sir."

Inside at last. Down a narrow runway. A sign.

FREAKS TO YOUR LEFT.

Turn. Turn. There!

"Ooohh, aren't they terrible! I can't look. What are they?

Ogling.

People pushing and the smell of antiseptic in the air where the freaks fall and fondle each other behind the invisible walls of the force field imprisoning them. Ruth Cameron stands and tries not to look at the people looking. She wears a brief and beaded costume that bares her breasts and leaves her white thighs naked. Behind her and a little to her right, stands Villane, dressed in a skintight black suit. He has dyed his eyes purple and curled his hair which sprouts from his head like a thick field of grass. He announces, as he mounts the platform, "From the far lands known only to the initiates come these freaks to entertain you. Watch and wonder, women and girls, you men who are not monsters. Nature's mirror has cracked. *Behold!*"

"Look! Look at that one there. What's it doing, hey?"

It's weeping.

"Oh, I'm glad we came, aren't you?"

"—hungry."

Villane: "—and ask yourselves as you cower in your beds at night, what manner of monsters are these? We cannot tell you. We do not know. We simply show you what lies beyond Man!"

Ruth: "Take home a filmette of freakdom. Only a quarter. Who'll buy? Who'll buy?"

She slips the coins into her girdle and passes out the filmettes in which monstrosities lie imprisoned.

Shrieking now in his plumed hat and flowing pantaloons, Adam York peddles gratification at his vendomat at the end of the runway. "Popcorn and peanut pills!" he cries. "Candy floss in a capsule. Try them. The delights of the godlings."

Children point fingers and loose brassy cries as they discover first this freak and then that one, each more thrilling than the last and each at once treasured by these young and innocent marauders in their new palace of pleasure.

On and on down the runway, past the freaks, through the crowd, beyond Adam York and his savory technological triumphs go the people seeking the circus.

They peer with excited eyes into the dispensos at the pictures of Sister in her pink tutu. *Cute.* They gaze at the gay butterflies on the ends of silken strings that flap their crimson wings and wink their yellow electric eyes and can be theirs for only ten cents.

"I want!" crow the children. "Get me!" they insist in raucous voices as indulgent parents, struck wild with the wonder of it all, buy, buy and never count the cost.

Into the main arena of the visitorium they flow like flotsam on a quaking sea to seat themselves, lean back and pop peanut pills into their mouths as the lights riot around them and the music sets their finger fluttering.

The gigantic clock set in the ceiling stares down like a jeweled eye and counts out time like a miser. Seven minutes to midnight. The people watch the minutes die and as the lights begin to fade, they shudder with anticipation in the sudden momentary darkness before the visitorium erupts in red luminescence and the clock screams midnight and Adam York bounds into the center ring in a new costume—a gilded coat and a tall tower of a hat, his feet slippered in silk and carrying a supple black ribbon of a whip and cries, "Citizens, *circus!*"

The music roars its wild refrain as York turns and points his whip imperiously at the entrance to the arena. In they come, the stumbling, shambling phantoms—the freaks. Like poorly constructed and badly manipulated marionettes they parade past York and the eyes of the audience. Hop. Grind. They cry out, some of them, mindless pleas or unfocused rage. The people stare and their hearts pound and their thousand eyes gorge themselves on horror. York's whip flicks through the air and lands on the blue-furred woman. She yelps and rises from her knees and hurries on and out through the exit after the others.

An unrecognizable Grandsir enters in their wake wearing the costume Ruth Cameron has made for him, a costume copied from his book about clowns. It is a garden of color, a carousel of polka dots—red, yellow, blue. Grandsir stands still for a long moment staring at the audience as if wondering who they are and who he is and what they all are doing here this dark and mysterious night. Behind the white paint, the flesh of his face is cold. Only his false, painted smile seems truly alive. His long moment ends as Gordon, wearing a glittering, spangled costume, scurries into the arena as York declares loud enough for all to hear, "Presenting, people, The Glorious Gordon, The Prince of Pain!" His whip cracks its signal and Gordon grabs the cable descending like a steel worm from the ceiling and is lifted up into the air and slowly whirled about the head of Grandsir who, remembering his role, throws back his ludicrously gloved hands in mock surprise, tilts from side to side in false dismay and pretends to swat ineffectually at this ignoble and annoying nuisance come to torment him.

Gordon waves the red and white striped baton he holds in his free hand, making sure that the audience sees it. Then he points it at Grandsir masquerading as King Carnival and a white flash of light flows out and crackles in the air. As it strikes Grandsir, he cries out in real pain and moves away. But the cable-carrying Gordon swings in a widening arc and Gordon, a bomb that cannot fall, points his baton again. The electricity leaps out at Grandsir. He yelps once more and now the audience knows what is happening and leans forward to get a better look. And laugh as Grandsir falls, gets up and runs with Gordon, an iridescent dragonfly, never far from him.

The audience becomes aware of Grandsir's irregular and strained breathing which is being amplified on the recordecks.

"Give him another one, kiddo!" screams a woman, leaning forward in her seat.

"Oh, oh!" cries Grandsir, playing his part, feeling his pain.

Laughter rises from the audience. The woman who screamed clutches at the arm of her husband sitting next to her, watching eagerly, her nails digging into the man's flesh. "There he goes!" she yells. "Get him again!"

Gordon does. *Crraacckkk!* Grandsir falls, stunned with the voltage. As the cable slows its motion, Gordon is twirled around in an ever-narrowing arc until his tiny feet touch the floor and he lets go of the cable to stand over the stricken clown at his feet. He gazes expectantly at the audience, points to the polka dotted heap at his feet and—

"The Glorious Gordon!" shouts York, reappearing in the arena.

Gordon bends and fastens the cable to the buckle on the belt hidden beneath Grandsir's costume. He raises his hands in triumph as the cable recoils into the ceiling above, carrying Grandsir up and away like a broken bird to vanish in the trap door overhead.

Applause.

Gordon bows and hops toward the exit where he turns and bows again and is gone.

"And now, Sister!" cries York. "See her come, see her go right before your astounded eyes. The miracle of the century! *Sister!*"

The music swells and soars, almost a parody of itself. All the lights dim except a single spotlight which throws down its pink pillar of light on nothing. Something! Sister suddenly appears in the light. She curtsies, her tutu a froth about her thin legs.

She does a little dance and the audience imagines her eyes are flirtatious and her stance coquettish. They are too far away to distinguish the cold glaze of hatred in her glance or the rigid muscles covering her small bones.

York wheels in a large metal box. He shows it to the audience, turns it, opens its door to reveal its emptiness.

He beckons to Sister who steps inside. He slams the door and snaps its lock and spins the box which is raised more than a foot off the floor on sturdy glass wheels. He taps the box twice with the butt of his whip, spins it again and proceeds to unlock the door.

Sister is gone.

Suddenly, a cry goes up from a man in the audience. Heads turn. *Sister!* Standing there beside the man who cried out, smiling her joyless smile. While the audience is straining to get a glimpse of her, York proceeds to lock the box once more.

"Hey, where'd she go?" the man cries.

York exclaims, "Matter melts before her. Chains cannot confine her. The magnificent Sister!" He ostentatiously opens the locked door and points triumphantly to Sister standing inside.

Ooohhs and aahhs float up from the throats of the audience.

This time, with the door still open, Sister vanishes again to reappear high above the heads of the audience in a revolving crystal globe where she floats in the vacuum of the globe like a lithe fish in an invisible sea. The audience claps its hands. Now Sister is gone from the globe. Now she is in the audience. Now astride York's shoulders, toppling his hat to the floor. Now back in the audience. Now nowhere to be seen.

She clings to Ruth who is sitting outside the arena on the runway awaiting the end of the performance. "A man," Sister sobs. "In there. He *touched* me!"

"Don't," Ruth says. "Don't cry." She wipes the oasis of tears from the desert of Sister's face. "It will soon be over. Now you'd better go back."

"Oh, I can't!" Sister says, knowing she can, knowing she must.

"It will soon be over," Ruth repeats, feeling helpless. She hugs Sister to her and the child's sobs subside. Suddenly, she is gone, leaving Ruth holding an armful of air.

"Here she is!" someone cries, and tries to seize Sister. It is becoming a game.

Sister appears beside York in the arena. "It's enough, isn't it? Please!"

York pats her shoulder. "Get ready for the finale."

Sister raises her arms and dances about on the metal platform hidden in the floor of the arena. She watches York who signals to Pume in his control room near the exit and a sudden burst of blue smoke rises up around Sister and the platform upon which she stands sinks into the floor and the floor closes over it as the smoke dissipates.

"And now," York announces, when the applause ends, "and now we present to you our feature and most fantastic attraction of the evening. The Funforall! At this very performance, some lucky citizen in the audience will be given a chance to enter the Funforall, spin the wheel of desire and dread, experience—" York pauses dramatically. "Experience," he continues, lowering his voice, "magic, marvels, miracles, mystery. He may meet horrors safely, delights joyously. Citizens, prepare! The Funforall!"

On cue, the complicated apparatus rises slowly out of the floor like some great behemoth, its brilliant lights instead of teeth flashing, its hundreds of integrated circuits instead of hair bristling.

"Now," York cries, "if you will check your tickets, I will read the number of the lucky winner." The audience waits as he rises to his full height and announces, "Y296L3."

"Me!" a man yells. "Over here. I win!"

"Come forward!" York commands.

The man picks his way among the rows of seats, reveling in the envious stares of his friends, a little frightened, thoroughly stimulated. When he reaches the floor of the arena and York, he stands slack-jawed and awed before the flashing, clicking, whirling Funforall.

There follows a whispered conference during which York determines that the man, although somewhat doubtful of the validity of York's claims for the Funforall, is willing, nevertheless, to give it a try.

The audience watches expectantly as the man steps inside the machine's transparent body and lies down in what resembles an upholstered tomb suspended from ropes wound with red ribbons in the center of the machine. They watch as York fastens thick straps around the man's body and binds his hands to the sides of the receptable that holds his body like a living corpse. York smears the man's skin in places—forehead, base of skull, tongue, inner ears and even more intimate places—with a slippery emerald oil after which he inserts the electrolytic pins. The man winces as the pins enter with a brief sting and blend with his flesh.

York surveys his subject and, satisfied, steps out of the machine, closes its door and turns again to confront the audience. "Fasten your fingers," he tells them, "to the receivers you will find in the arms of your chairs. By so doing, you will be able to experience a slightly diluted sensory feedback channeled to you through the man in the Funforall."

York selects a program spool almost at random and slips it into the slot in the side of the machine. He presses a button and the spool begins to spin. He sees the body of the man inside suddenly slump, each muscle grow flaccid. He simultaneously presses a switch and lowers a lever and the lights in the visitorium fade until only a faint luminosity remains in which the audience and even York himself seem like figures in a half-remembered dream.

The man inside the Funforall and each member of the audience grow limp and sightless as their minds leave the prisons of their bodies and fly back to the jeweled and tapestried tent of an imaginary Arabian sheik now buried in the cluttered closet of time. The spool spins soundlessly and the minds of the audience, freed, flit from body to body among the people in the hallucinatory tent and outside it, smelling, hearing, tasting . . .

. . . the juice of ripe figs stains the Sheik's chin and fingers as he lounges on his pile of bright pillows. He

draws on the water pipe at his side as the girls are brought in to him.

Nubile flesh, brown and yellow and white, passes before his feasting eyes. His jeweled finger points out that one there. And this small, shivering one. Rustle of silk. The whispered words of the slave trader in the Sheik's jaded ear tell of strange skills and stranger delights and devices worthy of a connoisseur. Smiles. A sighing wind, changing the patterns of the sand and of time itself. Acrid oil dripping from the lamps hanging from the tent poles. The glint of gold passing from hand to hand. Yellow on brown, brightening bitter black eyes. Night and the naked moon witness the truth spoken by the slave trader as the Sheik examines his purchases and tests their value. Colors, like paint dripping, rise and recede as flesh, like figs, is torn by teeth and little cries rip the fabric of the night beneath the billowing tent that is its own momentary heaven that hell has helped to create . . .

It ends as abruptly as it began. Moaning members of the audience shudder awake and touch themselves and their children, questions darting in their eyes and embarrassment mixed with pleasure prodding with the fingers of memory their mundane and familiar flesh.

Someone whispers and others hear. "Did you see that one with the ruby in her forehead? I felt—"

A woman groans under her burden of memory. "I thought it was terrible at first—him, I mean."

Indignantly, a woman tells her husband, "Do you think it's right for kids to see such stuff? Do you?"

York throws back the door of the machine and releases the bonds binding the man's body to the pallet in the center of the Funforall. He carefully ejects the electrolytic pins with the tip of his sharp knife and swabs the tiny exit wounds with a soothing elixir. As the man steps out, York waves him away and cries out to the audience, "Come back tomorrow night! Tomorrow night *you* could be the winner and experience sensory treasures *first-hand* with no secondary channel feedback. Tomorrow night, citizens! *Circus!*"

A week later, Grandsir looked up from the bed where he lay bundled in blankets as a knock sounded on his door. "Who?"

The door opened and Sister came into the room. "It's me," she announced.

"So I see."

"You sick or something?"

"No, just resting. I'm tired."

"Well," Sister said, "it's ten o'clock, you know. In two hours we've got to do it all over again."

"Don't remind me. That damned Gordon!"

"It's not just him. It's Pume who's to blame. Does it hurt a lot when he—?"

Grandsir nodded. He studied her as she moved aimlessly about the room, dragging her costume on the floor. He was about to chide her. Her tutu would get dirty. But did it matter, he wondered. Did anything really matter? He said nothing.

"Those people at the circus make me sick," Sister commented. She passed beside the bed, barely glancing at Grandsir.

He held out his hand and she took it as if she had been waiting for him to offer it. She let herself be drawn to the bed and she sat down on it as Grandsir hunched himself up on his pillow and covered her two hands with his own.

"I was thinking," she went on.

"About what? What were you thinking about?"

"What if one of them was mine?" Seeing his quizzical expression, she explained, "I mean what if one of the people at the circus was my father or my mother? One of the kids my brother maybe. I never knew them very well. I was pretty little when they got rid of me. But if one of them was, they probably wouldn't know me now, would they?"

"Probably not," Grandsir agreed, trying to think of a way to change the subject.

"No, I guess not." Sister shook her head and her hair caught the light in its cinnamon net. "Anyway, even if they did, they wouldn't let on, I suppose. I mean they wouldn't want me now either."

"What time is it?" Grandsir asked, feeling her warm hands in his like two tiny birds.

Sister ignored his question. "I don't care, I guess. I've got everything I need. A place to sleep and food and all. I've got you too."

Her defenses fell and Grandsir could only gather her to him as she wept, cursing an old man's helplessness. Rallying, he said, "Sure, you've got me. And I've got you and don't you forget it. We've got each other, Pume or no Pume. We're a team, we are."

Sister wrenched herself from his grasp and stood up quickly. "I'm not crying," she declared vehemently. "I hate kids who cry."

"I don't," was Grandsir's only comment. "Well," he said, throwing back his blankets, "time to get cracking."

"Yes. It's quarter past. See you later." Sister paused at the door. "Be careful tonight," she told Grandsir.

Grandsir sat for a moment on the edge of his bed after she had gone. Then he began to get ready. He sat down before the mirror and removed the lids from the jars of paint and began to become what he was not, a clown.

He was so engrossed in his task that he failed to hear Gordon as he opened the door and slid into the room. But he felt the sharp jab of electricity jar his spine and he stood up quickly, overturning his chair as he did so. Gordon grinned up at him, waving his candy-striped baton.

Grandsir snarled, "Get out of here, you filthy little beast, before I stomp you like a bug!"

Gordon's smile disappeared. He flicked his baton again and the electricity crackled in the still air of the room. Grandsir suppressed a cry of pain. He advanced toward Gordon and an uninformed observer would have registered shock at the sight of a clown in polka dots and painted smile advancing on what looked like a harmless, helpless child. But the same observer, if possessed of keener eyes and sharper sensibilities, would have seen the chilling fear in the clown's eyes and noted the fact that the childlike creature before him did not cower or shrink from him but, rather, seemed to welcome him as the cat welcomes the bird hopping toward its slavering jaws.

"Get out!" Grandsir cried.

Gordon's thoughts were a sudden awful onslaught. *"Maybe I'll kill you tonight. I could. I might. They'd like that. Watch out, old fool! Watch out!"*

The baton again. Gordon's exit coincided with Grandsir's anguished cry. When he was alone again, Grandsir surrendered to the weakness that was washing about him like mountainous waves. He sat down on the bed and dropped his head into his hands, unmindful of the smeared makeup that covered his bony fingers. He pitied himself and hated himself for doing so. But he felt so full of years. He felt betrayed by the weakness of his ancient body that could still suffer pain and, because of this sad fact, force an old man who had always wanted only books and gardens to do things that made his brain nauseous and his heart want to vomit. He forcibly rejected these thoughts because he remembered that, though no brave centaurion, he was nevertheless, by his own choice, responsible for Sister. She had no one. He had only himself. So the clown that was Grandsir laughed and laughed as he thought how absurd it all was—himself and his shaky valor, the circus, even Cityside itself.

He hastily repaired his makeup, zipped up his costume and went out in the hall to meet the world. He met Ruth Cameron.

"Hello, Grandsir," she said. "I guess we're all ready now."

"Oh," he said, "I'd give my right arm and left leg, young woman, if I could drop a few of these years of mine that I've really no further use for. You look so lovely!"

Ruth smiled. He was always so cheerful, she thought. So pleasant and quick with compliments. She wondered how he managed it. Didn't he ever worry or fret or fear? She wanted to ask him what his secret was but she didn't. It would sound so silly and maybe he didn't even know he had a secret. "Come along," she said, taking his arm.

They went into the living room where they found Villane and York already waiting.

"Pume's gone on ahead with Gordon," Villane said. "He left an aeroauto for us."

"Where's Sister?" York asked.

"Here." She materialized in the room.

"Then we're ready," Villane said.

They rode down together in the tube and went outside where they found the aeroauto hovering on its cushion of air, its doors open. They got in. Villane took the controls and they glided through the brightly lighted streets that were alive with Priestmen at each corner and scores of people heading for the visitorium.

"Our fans," commented York wryly, indicating the people thronging along with them.

"It's funny," Villane mused.

"What's funny?" York asked.

"We're do-gooders. That's what we are. If Pume's theory is correct, although I wouldn't vouch for its validity just yet, we'll help to abolish the Dump. Bring sanity back to Cityside."

"Sanity!" York snorted contemptuously. "You're confusing sanity with fantasy. We're not so much do-gooders as we are providers of placebos."

"What's placebos?" Sister asked from her seat beside Grandsir.

"A sort of sugar pill," York told her. "What I mean, Villane, is that we're just providing a way of going insane on the installment plan. The people get their kicks from the circus now, sure. But will it last? Or will it just be a case, as I said, of insanity eventually anyway. If not today, surely tomorrow. If not tomorrow, well, the day after will do."

"There's nothing wrong with circuses actually," Villane ventured.

"Speak for yourself!" Grandsir snapped.

"Sorry, Grandsir. I'll qualify that. There's nothing wrong with circuses without Gordons."

Grandsir muttered to himself.

Villane went on. "Pume figures the people need a chance to forget about Landsend."

"Circuses won't conquer Landsend," Grandsir declared testily. "Don't know but that Landsend might be better than the Dump even," he mused.

"Don't talk like that!" Ruth said.

"Don't you tell me how to talk, whippersnapper! When you get to be my age, you'll see things a lot different."

So, Ruth thought. He's not all honey and roses after all. Oddly, she felt relieved. She couldn't bring herself to pity the old man but she did wonder if he wasn't right about Landsend. She looked at Villane, at his strong jaw jutting forward over the controls of the aeroauto and thought *young*. Him, me, York and Sister certainly. Landsend means one unwanted thing to us—death. To Grandsir, she speculated, it may mean peace and an end to pain. "Sorry, Grandsir," she said softly.

"Nothing to be sorry about," he said. But he couldn't help adding, "Or everything."

Sister squeezed his hand.

Villane concentrated on the controls of the aeroauto, wishing he could forget about circuses and knowing he could not.

They arrived at the visitorium some minutes later and went inside, leaving the aeroauto in the hands of a burly attendant who had been clearly impressed by their costumes and the fact that, in his limited world, they were definitely celebrities and entitled to a particularly oily slice of the servile respect he automatically doled out to his customers.

Villane left the others and, accompanied by Ruth, went down to the lower level where the freaks were imprisoned in their pens. He switched on the lights and forced himself to face them. The one with the wings, he noted, seemed to be slowing down. Its eyes opened seldom and it was obviously losing muscle tone. He would have to take it back after this performance for another treatment in Pume's laboratory.

Ruth busied herself with the feedings. Villane, watching her, thought she was becoming very expert. But at a price. She showed no outward sign of disgust or dismay as she went about spooning the food into the gaping, drooling mouths. But neither did she show any compassion or any faint hint of tenderness. She showed no emotion at all. And that, Villane decided, was probably worse than an honest expression of disgust. But, perhaps, a necessary defense. Did she, he wondered, see in the freaks the products of the Nursery? Probably not. Because they —the Limbos—were usually ugly, defaced and violent where the freaks could be considered simply interesting, even amusing, if one did not know the nature of their origin and could avoid thinking of them as human. Villane found himself admiring the curve of Ruth's thighs and the promise of her bared breasts and he felt an almost forgotten drive of desire surge through his body and alight in his loins. He tried to avoid the words that came but they would not be denied—*need, love, want*. Like marbles they rolled in his mind and like marbles they careened off one another chaotically. I need her, he thought. I want her, he admitted to himself. The other word must wait for a more auspicious time.

"Help me, Phillip," Ruth said. "This one's so weak."

He struggled up out of his reverie and the fish of his desire sank back into its dark lake. They managed, with Villane holding the freak's knobbed head, and Ruth deftly inserting the spoon between its bulbous lips, to get it to swallow a little. Ruth wiped its naked chest and shoulders when they had finished and then they left the pen together.

Upstairs, Ruth took her place with Villane as the attendants herded the freaks into place behind them. They could hear the music blaring from the arena and they could see York at the end of the runway behind his refreshment stand.

When the doors were opened to admit the people, Villane began his spiel and Ruth offered her filmettes. It seemed to them both that they were seeing the same people, hearing the same words spoken, sensing the same reactions. The people flowed past them in a rippling stream until at last the stream dried up and the raucous music and brightening lights from the arena signaled the beginning of another performance. Ruth and Villane left their platform and went to stand, side by side, in the entrance, watching.

Villane watched the attendants herd the freaks into the arena. When they had come and gone and York had announced Gordon and Grandsir, Villane turned to find Sister standing beside him. "He's too old to do that stuff," Sister remarked, her eyes on Grandsir stumbling about in the arena. It sounded to Villane like a plea. But what, if anything, did Sister think he could do about it? As Grandsir suffered the torments of Gordon, Sister teleported away.

Villane wished there was something he could do. Maybe the old man was right. For him, Landsend might be better than this humiliating and harmful torture at the hands of Gordon.

Villane heard the sudden shouts but at first he could not distinguish either their meaning or their purpose. He listened carefully.

"Get him outa there!"

"Bring on the Funforall!"

A refrain then, rising and falling like great flapping wings. "We want the Funforall! The Funforall! The Funforall!"

York, in the arena, seemed confused. He gestured helplessly at Pume in the control booth and Pume signaled to Grandsir who hurried out of the arena. Simultaneously, Gordon dropped from his cable and ran after Grandsir, pelted by peanut pills and assaulted by the derisive hoots and howls of the angry audience.

"We want the Funforall!"

In desperation, York introduced Sister. She appeared. The crowd grew quiet. What, they wondered, was this new thing, this cute little girl thing? Sister disappeared. She reappeared among the members of the audience. The

75

crowd did not care. They took up their refrain again, only louder and more insistent this time.

At last, York surrendered to their demands. He whispered to Sister. She nodded and vanished. York stepped aside as the Funforall rose slowly out of a cave in the floor and the crowd roared their noisy approval.

York immediately read the winning number. Instantly, several voices were raised, declaring themselves to be winners. York raised his hands and pleaded for silence. Sulkily, the audience quieted briefly as two men and a woman rose and approached him, their tickets held firmly in their hands. As York examined the tickets, he saw to his surprise that the numbers on each of the tickets was the same and that each matched the winning number he had just announced which had been given to him by Pume.

"We will have a short intermission," he told the audience as firmly as he could manage although he did not feel very firm either in his resolve or his ability to carry out that resolve.

"No!" bellowed the single voice of the crowd. "The Funforall! Now!"

York realized that he had no choice. "One at a time then. You first."

The woman he had picked stepped into the transparent cubicle and lay down, blushing as York inserted the electrolytic pins. He stepped out of the machine, chose a small spool labeled *Eighteenth Century, France* and activated the Funforall . . .

. . . the French court erupted in the minds housed in the suddenly limp bodies of the woman and the members of the audience. There was dancing amid the sweet smell of powder on shoulders and wigs. Swans glided wetly across the lake outside the palace while warm candles flickered in many windows high above the heads of the swans and the dancers. The cries from the grimy streets of Paris were only a memory in the minds of the courtiers lying deep with their lovers who smiled politely . . .

"She's had enough!" insisted one of the two men waiting. "It's my turn now."

When the two men had gone and returned—one to Earth War Three and the other to the Nursery—they and the people in the audience accepted York's announcement that the circus was ended with reluctance and something of the sadness of punished children whose toys have been hidden from them. They filed out along the runway where Ruth tried in vain to sell them her filmettes of freakdom, past Villane who silently noted their flushed and eager faces and their hot eyes, and they said . . .

"—wish it coulda been me."

"Well, maybe you'll be lucky tomorrow night. You wanna come back tomorrow night?"

"I'll say! Why, sure!"

. . . while Pume listened as he mingled with the departing crowd and let his brain flame and ideas flare phoenixlike in its furnace.

Later, talking to York in the living room of his apartment, Pume said, "A most remarkable development, wouldn't you say?"

"Unexpected, certainly," York replied. "By the way, Pume, why were there three winners tonight? I thought there was supposed to be only one a night."

Pume smiled. "An experiment of mine. I was quite impressed with the growing interest in our Funforall during the past week of performances. The people seem to enjoy it, wouldn't you agree? So I wanted to see what would happen if three people won. I arranged it. It does one important thing. It varies the entertainment during the evening. Why, consider tonight, for example. We visited the Nursery, went to war and enjoyed French history." He tapped his fingers on the table.

"It seems to me that you've got problems, Pume. Your circus idea is beginning to fall apart. You saw how they weren't interested in Grandsir or Sister. All they wanted was the Funforall. To turn a phrase, to twist it a bit, your mouse has labored and brought forth a mountain."

"Ah, York, but what a mountain it is! Think about it for a moment. Think of the possibilities hiding like rich veins of ore in this mountain of mine."

"All I see is lines of people waiting to climb your mountain."

"Precisely, precisely," Pume chortled. "Lines of people. Thousands. We started—I did—with a simple hypothesis. Our citizens needed something to take their minds off the strain they were under because of daily Defense and Deterrence pressures and the like. So I created the circus. It is a success, you'll have to admit, if not quite in the fashion I expected. But the hypothesis has been proven valid as you've seen. Only certain variables in that hypothesis can now be permanently discarded."

"What you're saying then," York prompted, "if I understand you correctly, is that all you now need is the Funforall. The Funforall *is* your circus now, all wrapped up in a neat mechanical package."

"You deserve a great deal of the credit."

York rose and crossed the room. Turning back to Pume, he said, "I don't want any credit, not for taking sensation and peddling it like a gaudy toy to misfits and potential psychotics and worse. No, Pume, I give the credit all to you."

"Not so fast!" Pume snapped. "Please do not lose sight of your position here. Do not lose sight of the value of what we are doing. You're free to go now. But send Grandsir to me."

"The old man's tired," York protested. "He's probably in bed already."

"York, I said now!"

Pume watched York go and then he raised his arms high above his head and stretched luxuriously. Like a great bear, he yawned and let his hands come down to rest on his stomach while he waited for Grandsir. He heard him coming, grumbling down the hall.

"I got to get some sleep, Pume, or I'm going to go *phhtt* like a busted balloon."

"Oh, shut up and listen to me! Tomorrow—today, actually, you will begin a new research project. You will no longer be confined to circuses. I'm about to broaden your heretofore limited horizons. I want to know *everything* about the past, all its stories and people and events and comings and goings."

"Why, that would take forever!" Grandsir exclaimed.

"It won't. It mustn't. Because we're in a new and, I think, a much more profitable business than we ever could have hoped for. We're going to sell pieces of the past to all our citizens equally and without discrimination or favor to insure their well-being and the continued survival of Cityside. Get books, old man! Get going!"

When Grandsir had gone, shaking his head, Pume studied the vistas opening up in his mind. Worlds, not to conquer, but to peddle. As he did so, the profane words of the crazed psyche in the Disposal Depot cried out again in his mind: *"Screw Cityside!"*

The remembered blasphemy infuriated Pume and he vowed again that he would save Cityside whatever the cost. He had plans. His Priestmen would be needed, of course. They could be counted on. The Council would have to be persuaded but that would be easy. And he had already decided upon the roles that would be played by all of his puppet people now so uneasily asleep in their beds all around him.

In the days and weeks that followed, Pume busied himself with the details of his plan. He sat with the other members of the Council in a second special session where he reported on the success of his circus. He told them that he believed experience was the best teacher, as the Priestman pointed out, and that it was perfectly obvious that the circus as originally conceived was already, in part, obsolete. Over their expressions of concern, he explained that this did not mean failure but rather a different brand of success. The people, he said, had chosen for themselves. It was that simple. They wanted not Sister, not clowns, not freaks or other simplistic entertainments. They wanted sensation. Understandable, Pume insisted, when one considered the difficulties of D & D, etcetera. The members of the Council nodded their heads and stroked their chins and decided Pume had something there for certain. What, then, did he suggest?

Pume told them his eyes firing with the light of prophesy. He urged that the visitorium be remodeled according to his specifications and that it be called Sensory Central. He recommended that citizens be allowed to use Sensory Central on the basis of their success in achieving their production quotas plus their scores during Allegiance Alerts. He proposed that these evaluations and the entire administration of Sensory Central be placed in the hands of the Priestmen under his guidance, as he so casually phrased it. He outlined the benefits and cataloged advantages. When all the chin stroking and head scratching was finished, his plan was approved as he had known it would be.

It was approved partly because he had had the good sense and foresight to speak privately to several members of the Council in advance of the formal meeting and promise each of them certain rewards. Since few of them knew anything at all about the history of that other world that had existed before Earth War Three and the eventual birth of Cityside, the wonders he spoke of were tempting. His work was helped also by the fact that his confidants had attended one or more of the circus performances and were, although basically quite unimaginative, not without the capacity to appreciate the delights that Pume could make available to them—and without fee—under his proposed new program.

So they voted for something they did not fully understand, not quite, but nudged on by Pume's winged words ricocheting about the corridors of their minds.

Pume proceeded to let his contracts and study architect's plans. He signed his name here and he issued orders there. The population of Cityside grew as full of rumors as of food. There was talk of private Funforalls for each citizen. Someone had heard that the alterations of the visitorium now being made had something to do with an expected attack from Landsend. Someone else emphatically insisted that only citizens whose last names began with M were to be allowed inside the new visitorium.

Pume, when the alterations of the visitorium were finally completed, made a tour of inspection with two of his top level Priestmen.

"A veritable temple!" gushed the taller of the two as they walked past the tiers of rectangular compartments.

They entered the control center on the ground level where three walls were covered with the segmented control panel that Phillip Villane and Adam York had designed to Pume's specifications.

Pume declared, "Here is where the heart is. Here is where the programing will be done. Note that each compartment in each tier is identifiable on the panel by its particular code symbol. It is from here that the level and intensity of sensory impressions will be disseminated and monitored. And over here," he continued, beckoning to the two Priestmen, "are the physio-terminals where specimen's temperature, bone tension, blood composition and other items can be measured and controlled."

"Then it will be perfectly safe?" questioned one of the Priestmen.

"Yes," Pume answered. "If a specimen becomes too highly stimulated by, say, an excess of adrenalin it will show up here in terms of changing blood composition. Then the program can be either modified or halted altogether."

"Praises!" breathed the Priestmen in unison.

Then the taller of the two asked, "What are we to tell the people about this new marvel?"

"Summon all Priestmen to a special service to be held in the Interrogation Vault at Headquarters. Then and there will I answer your question and any and all others that might exist in the minds of the brethren after I speak to them of the future."

The Priestmen made the safety sign, bowed and left the visitorium.

Alone, Pume strolled about the room, admiring the remarkable handiwork of so many that had been guided by his brain. Landsend would never conquer Cityside, he vowed. Not now! Every nerve fiber in his body tingled and victory and triumph flowed like the blood in his veins through every cell of his body.

With evident reluctance, he left the visitorium that was now Sensory Central and commandeered a passing aeroauto which took him to the headquarters of his Priestmen in the center of Cityside. He went into the building and felt the gloom settle on his shoulders like a heavy mantle. As he passed the Training Room, he paused briefly to listen with pleasure to the litany of the fledgling Priestmen in the early stages of their development.

"Good is good and bad is bad. Better believe, better believe. To believe is better. Better is best. Best to be good for Cityside!"

When he arrived in the Interrogation Vault, he found that the barren stone room was filled with kneeling Priestmen, their faces hidden beneath the cowls burying their bowed heads. Pume threaded his way through the throng, assiduously avoiding the circular pits in the floor where offenders were placed during their interrogation and ignoring the familiar Lessons lettered on the walls which stated unequivocally that *"All's well that works well"* and *"Might's right"* and *"The best is."*

Pume mounted the podium in the front of the dimly lighted room. "I am Supreme Priestman Pume," he declared ritualistically, beginning the meeting.

"Our leader," droned the Priestmen.

"Your brother."

"Our voice."

Heads were raised to Pume, eyes hidden in shadowy faces.

"You are to play a new and rewarding role in the continued effort to save Cityside," Pume told them. "Each of you will have an opportunity to continue turning citizens toward Truth. Each of you will continue, but in new and miraculous ways, to reduce Error. As your leader and one who loves you and your work among our citizens, I say to you with joy in my heart that you are present at the dawning of a new day."

Pume hurried on, describing Sensory Central, how he had conceived it, what it was designed to do for weary citizens, how the Priestmen would be in complete control of its administration and its output. He told them they must search their own hearts and the hearts of their brother Priestmen and, most especially, the hearts of the sometimes wayward citizens who too often failed to see the Error they committed when they failed to produce sufficient toxic materials in the Life Laboratory or refused through confusion or fear to serve as breedettes. Pume pleaded for pity for these misguided ones but demanded their correction. The task ahead, he assured the Priestmen, was bound to be easier. He spoke of carrots and sticks, of rabbits and hounds and bluntly of bribes and their correlation with the behavior of citizens. He told the Priestmen that they were to continue to be masters, kindly and concerned, of the citizens and that they would from this moment on absorb into their File of Functions the organization formerly known as Reality Creation and Control.

Pume waited until the cheers died away before he spoke again. "Priestmen are you. Masters of the sanity of this sovereign state and its citizens. Mind makers! Mentality and morality, I say to you, and you know I speak the truth, are inseparable. Indeed, one feeds upon the other. When one sickens, the death of the other is not far off. From you as fountainhead will flow the benefits of Sensory Central to the minds of our citizens. Mastery is yours!"

"Praises!" shouted the Priestmen.

"This I ask of you," Pume said, beginning the end of the familiar ritual. "Who must be hated?"

"The enemy."

"Who is he, this hider?"

"Landsend is he."

"What must we do against him?"

"Defend and deter."

Pume raised his hands and his hearers quieted although many still shook with ecstasy and others made the safety sign over and over again like figures in a filmfax that has sprung its sprockets, allowing the same image to flick on and off, on and off. "We will now tour Sensory Central and all will be revealed to you. Your roles will be assigned. Your duties defined. Training will begin at once. Shifts will be extended to a full twenty hours. It will be necessary for each of you to take sustenance shots during indoctrination and training in order that your bodies may be aided in obeying your wills. And each of you will be given an opportunity to experience for himself what lies beyond the veil of the control center in Sensory Central so that you may gain wisdom and understanding and may thus be in a sound and sturdy position to maintain your mastery in this most delicate and necessary venture. Priestmen, I salute you!"

Villane walked from one end of the living room to the other and then back again like the stiff pendulum of a metronome ticking off the measurements of the room. His face was tense and occasionally he wiped a hand across his eyes. Ruth sat watching him, as if waiting for something to happen just as she had been doing throughout the past month.

York wandered aimlessly into the room, shattering the silence. "We eat and drink, friends, why not be merry?"

"I'll tell you why not," snapped Villane, halting his pacing. "Because of what is happening. Because of what we have helped happen. Do you know what I did this morning, York?"

York shook his head, studying Villane.

"I killed! I killed the freaks. Pume ordered me to do it and, by God, I did it!"

Ruth said, "You didn't *kill* them. You simply let them die."

Villane said, "Don't play with words. I pulled the implants and they died. In ten minutes the floor was covered with filthy gangrenous matter. It wasn't pretty, I can assure you. Merry, York? You must be crazy!"

York gave Villane a sad smile. "It might be worth a try."

Villane resumed his pacing. He talked as he walked. "I can't help wondering where all this is leading. What will it mean to us? Pume hasn't said anything about us or bothered us since the circus ended."

"That's not quite true," Ruth corrected. "You and York designed the control systematics for Sensory Central."

"Well, yes," Villane admitted. "But that's not what I mean. I mean Pume hasn't asked us to do anything else and that's what worries me—not knowing what's next."

"What you don't know won't hurt you," York said.

"You sound like a Priestman," Villane told him sharply. He wondered how York managed to maintain such an air of calm composure in the face of what was happening. He had said he was afraid of pain. Villane understood that. But York seemed to be actually enjoying himself. The man was a contradiction. On the one hand, he deliberately refused to continue with his work in Reality Creation and Control and on the other he now laughed at and ridiculed not only himself but the rest of them as well. "Everything seems so fantastic," Villane mused, remembering the circus and the pattern of his own life.

"For all intents and purposes," York said, "fantasy and fact are inseparably linked. Today you imagine you'd like to go to the circus. Tomorrow you go. Could the second happen without the first?"

"I don't understand you. There's a definite difference between reality and fantasy. One *is* and the other *is not*."

"And I claim, Villane," York insisted, "that one can't always tell which is which."

"I can! Wanting to go to the circus, to use your example, is not at all the same thing as going to the circus."

"Villane, look at it this way. If I wear a ring with a red stone in it and you ask me if the stone is a ruby and I tell you that yes, it definitely is because I believe it is, then for me at least the stone is a ruby simply because I *believe* it is."

"I think I see his point," Ruth commented. "What a person believes is so, *is* so for that person at that time. I never thought of it quite that way but it makes sense."

"Smart girl," York said.

She was, Villane thought. Smart. And attractive. It was her attractiveness, he realized, that made him wish she were not—well, one of them. Like Sister, she seemed so defenseless. It was different for York. He looked strong and that, somehow, made it seem all right. And me, Villane asked himself. What about me? He decided it didn't matter. He heard Ruth greet Grandsir as he came into the room with his arms full of books.

"Pume's got plans," Grandsir announced.

"Tell us something new," York commented, dropping into a chair and beginning to examine his blunted fingernails with assiduous concern.

"No, I mean *new* plans," Grandsir said.

"What kind of plans?" Villane asked, feeling anxiety flutter in the center of his stomach. Silently, he cursed his lack of courage that made each new day a thing of dread, an ambush holding unknown enemies.

"Well," said Grandsir, "he told me I can't work fast enough. Can't get through enough books or record enough data fast enough to suit him. Besides, he says, he's got a more efficient way of managing things. Thanks to York."

"What have you got to do with it?" Ruth asked York.

"Oh, everything!" Grandsir stated. "Tell them, boy."

York looked up. "I just told Pume what he already knew. For a man who thinks he's so smart, he's actually pretty blind to what lies before his eyes."

"Get to the point," Villane said.

"The point is simply this. I told Pume that it would be a lot more efficient if he simply made use of the resources he has on hand."

"Ha!" snorted Grandsir.

"What resources?" Ruth asked.

"Why, us, of course," York answered.

Villane had known it was coming and now it was here. His stomach sank and his hands began to sweat. "Us?"

"Us," York repeated. "He'll use our minds and our memories. Our loves and hates and hungers. Together we represent a kind of mother lode of facts and fantasies that could fill a good hundred program spools or more."

"He means," said Grandsir, "that Pume is going to steal our ideas and feelings and like that."

Ruth's hand rose to touch her forehead. She seemed to be feeling the pulse of her mind beating and seeking a way to protect it from Pume's planned invasion.

Villane, watching her, suspected she was feeling the same uneasiness that needled him at the moment.

"But what can *we* give Pume?" Ruth asked.

Sister materialized in the room. "A kick in the shins," she said.

Ruth, startled by Sister's sudden appearance and her answer, burst into giggles.

"Forthright little thing, isn't she?" York commented with a grin. "I'd like to give him something a bit more than merely a kick in the shins. Anyone got a gun?"

The question shocked them all into a clearer awareness of their plight in relation to Pume. Villane saw that York's expression had changed. His face had lost its look of amused tolerance and had hardened into a granite mask. Villane felt once again the flow of power that emanated from York and that could not be accounted for purely on the basis of his massive body. There was more. Certain strange fires raged in that body, Villane guessed. Perhaps York's assumed nonchalance was merely a defense against dark impulses driving the man.

"We couldn't kill Pume, could we?" Ruth whispered.

York shrugged and remained silent.

Sister wanted to know what was going on. She addressed her question to all of them but it was Grandsir who answered.

"We're in for another bit of a go with Pume," he told her. "Pume wants to fiddle with our minds—"

Villane, interrupting, said, "While Cityside burns."

"And what's that supposed to mean, boy?" Grandsir asked. Then, understanding the reference, he said, "Not bad. Not good either. True, though."

"Will it hurt, do you think?" Sister asked in a small voice.

Villane realized she had voiced the thought that was in all of their minds at the moment. One of the thoughts. He heard Ruth rush in with reassurance.

"No, Sister," Ruth said, without really knowing. "It won't hurt. I'm sure of that."

Sister glanced at her and then at Grandsir as if seeking confirmation of the truth of Ruth's statement. Grandsir said nothing. "Dammit all!" Sister exclaimed and vanished.

They floundered in a sea of silence for several minutes after Sister had gone. No one knew quite what to say. Sister's epithet had expressed the deep despair that they all felt but were too weak or too strong to state.

"Ruth's right, actually," York said at last. "It doesn't hurt. Not in any physical sense."

"In what sense then?" Villane asked.

"Not any, necessarily. It's just that it leaves one feeling rather drained. There's an obsolete phrase, incidentally, that describes the process. Invasion of privacy, I think it was."

"But what's wrong with that?" Villane wanted to know.

York glared at him. His words, when they came, were sharp and his tone insulting. "You have listened too long to the Priestmen, Villane." York quoted their familiar slogan, " 'Every man's thoughts are his brother's.' Once upon a time," York continued, "once upon a much earlier time, the phrase 'invasion of privacy' defined a kind of crime committed against a private citizen. And that's another phrase you've never heard, I'll wager. *Private* citizen. Now, as you know, we are all *public* citizens. There's a big difference."

Villane found the idea fascinating. *Private* citizen. "It may not be so bad," he suggested a moment later, fully expecting that it would be.

"We'll know soon enough, I expect," York said, rising. He left the room.

"Wait," Grandsir called, hurrying after him. "You're to read this book, Pume says."

When Grandsir returned to the room, he plopped his pile of books down on the table. He chose one and handed it to Villane. "Yours."

Villane read the title: *Les Miserables*.

Ruth took the book Grandsir handed her. It was a copy of *Madame Bovary*. She leafed idly through the pages and then stood up and headed for the door. "I'll see to Sister."

Grandsir shook his head. "Years ago, I used to say I wondered what the world was coming to. But I never did dream—" He left the sentence unfinished, still shaking his head.

"We're alive and healthy," Villane offered. "That's something."

Grandsir picked up his book and gave Villane a look of contempt. "Boy," he said, "you don't know anything at all."

We're like animals attacking one another, Villane thought, when Grandsir had gone. Only animals wouldn't act like this. Not to their own kind. He looked down at his book as he listened to the soft clicking of the serviset in the wall and hearing the almost inaudible hissing of the floor vents and he wondered how such a clean and comfortable room could hold such terrors. Then he realized that the terrors were not in this room surrounding him but inside his own mind, that other room with a thousand locked doors and so few keys.

Ruth returned.

Villane knew she was standing in the doorway watching him but he gave no sign. He waited to see what she would do, what she might say. Had she known he was alone, he asked himself. Was that why she had come back? She must be feeling that hollow loneliness that had long ago overwhelmed him. Did she too, he wondered, hoping, want someone to touch her forehead, caress her cheek and whisper gentle words in her ear?

"Sister wouldn't let me in," Ruth said at last.

Villane looked up, affecting surprise at seeing her standing there. "Why?"

Ruth crossed the room and sat down in a chair facing him. "Why? I don't know. But I think she's frightened."

"Of you?"

"No, not of me. But she's gone into hiding. Maybe she hopes whatever it is she's afraid of will just go away. I don't think it will. In fact, I'm sure it won't."

"The trouble is we have so few alternatives."

"Yes, I know."

Villane studied her now that she was no longer looking directly at him but gazing across the room into space. "Would you like a drink?"

She didn't reply at first and Villane repeated his question as he stood up and went to the serviset.

"Something strong," she said.

He brought her the glass of liquor and watched as she swallowed a large part of it as if in the grip of a terrible thirst. "Careful with that stuff," he warned her. "It's pretty rocky."

Her fingers had touched his as he handed her the glass. An accident?

"I feel pretty rocky," she said.

"I understand."

"It's not enough."

The implication in her statement seemed clear to Villane. But, he cautioned himself, it may seem clear only because he wanted it to be. He said, "It's late."

Ruth stood up, avoiding his eyes. He followed her out of the room and down the corridor. They stopped at the door to her quarters which bore the painted legend: CAMERON. Like a cage. "Good night," she said softly.

Villane took a step toward her but she opened the door and closed it behind her.

In bed, Villane lay looking at the ceiling he could not see and waited for sleep to come. When it did not, he switched on the pencil thin beam of light in the headboard of his bed, picked up the copy of *Les Miserables* and began to read. Later, when sleep finally did arrive, he drifted, dreaming of loaves of bread and the sound of shattering glass and running footsteps and he heard the shouts of his pursuers and the cries of his starving children and smelled the dankness and moisture in his gloomy prison cell that turned into the walls of Pume's apartment as he breathed in and out, sane and singular in his soft bed.

Not everyone slept that night. Pume didn't. York didn't. They sat together in York's quarters and they discussed Pume's plans. No discussion, really. Rather, Pume talked and told York what must be done and what he would do and York listened.

"You were more than right," Pume stated. "York, you were marvelous. Cityside needs men like you. But, to get to specifics. I've been thinking over what you said. Grandsir is a gold mine. He's old and he's seen things—lived through a lot. Why, he even knows about the time before Earth War Three. He'll be good for a long while. Then, there's Sister. Now at first I couldn't see what good Sister would be to me since she's so young and relatively inexperienced. But once I got to thinking it over, I realized that what at first had seemed to me to be a distinct disadvantage is in reality a tremendous *ad*vantage."

"I thought you'd catch on to that fact," York commented, sitting stiffly on the edge of his bed.

"Sister's got a mind that isn't all mixed up with our conditioned attitudes and ways of looking at things. Sister's mind is relatively untouched and who knows what she might be able to give us for the programs."

"Then you've got Villane and Ruth—"

"Ah, yes, those two. Interesting possibilities there. I think you might investigate the installation of a circuit link between the two of them when we record. Who knows what might develop if they are properly connected and attuned. One program, two points of view."

York said, "And there's me."

"Yes, you. We'll discuss you later, shall we? No need to rush things too fast, is there?" Pume sighed and slumped down in his chair. "Oh, York, it feels so good to know that one is doing what must be done and what one is doing is truly worthwhile. You understand, don't you? In fact, you are probably the only one who understands. I suppose I can't expect the same depth of perception or the same degree of cooperation from the others. Gordon is no help in such delicate matters. That's not to say he hasn't his proper place." Pume sighed and stretched, beaming at York. "Oh, York, you and I are going to be the salvation of Cityside!"

The protest that was rising to York's lips sought to struggle free of his mouth, sought to make his hands move, to shake his head in a negative declaration. But he subdued it. The slight bulge that he could never avoid noticing beneath Pume's robe might have been a viper poised to strike, so threatening did it seem to him. Before the hidden threat it represented, York's powerful body melted like a thick icicle and his will turned to water. And to Pume's service.

"—try to see it my way, York," Pume was saying. *"Our* way. Because we all want the same thing. The protection of our beloved Cityside and peace. York, please! Don't look at me like that. I act from selfless motives. Moral motives! I want only good things. Try to understand that."

York nodded. "The end must justify the means, is that it?"

"Put it that way if you choose. You can't deny the value of the end and if the means to achieve it prove to be, at times, not always to our liking, we must nevertheless push on with our eyes always fixed on that worthy end. It's what keeps me going."

"I want to get some sleep."

Pume, momentarily lost in his thoughts, did not reply.

"Pume, I said I have to get some sleep."

Pume abandoned his reverie. He smiled at York. "Of course." He pulled a tiny box from his pocket and flipped its lid open. "Here."

York took the shining capsule and promptly swallowed it. He lay down on his bed. Instantly, he slept.

Pume stared down at him, despising him. What did such a man know about values? Although he had tried and tried to explain it to him, Pume knew that York did not truly understand. He did not really care. He did not care about Cityside the way Pume did. His eyes were blind to the beauty Pume saw in its arsenals and towers and heat fields. Pume spoke aloud in the stillness of the room. "You, York, are as helpless as Sister, as any of the rest of them, and it is good that you know it and act accordingly." The familiar urge gripped Pume and he did not try to resist it. He located York's button on his little box and he pressed it. He listened with pleasure to York's drugged cry and watched him shudder in his sleep.

The next day, Pume breakfasted with gusto. He laughed aloud over something Gordon thought at him and he urged the others at the table with him—Ruth, Villane and Grandsir—to show a little life and stop looking so full of woe. His admonitions failed in their purpose except in Gordon's case. After he had finished eating Gordon scampered about the room like an agitated mouse because Pume had promised him that he would be allowed to listen to the spools that he got from each of the others. Pume, looking about the room, asked, "Where is Sister? Sleeping still?"

Ruth dropped her gaze and Villane busied himself with his knife and fork. Grandsir looked away.

"Get her," Pume ordered, addressing Grandsir.

He rose obediently and left the room. When he returned some minutes later, Sister accompanied him. Ruth felt relief at the sight of her and she raised her hand in greeting. "Good morning, Sister," she called, as brightly as she could manage.

"Morning," Sister said, seating herself as far away from Pume as she could manage. She studied the faces of the people at the table as if seeking a missing piece of a difficult puzzle. She ate a little and that little with evident effort.

"Gordon," Pume said, "wake our good friend York, if you will."

"No need," said York, as he came into the room, his face pale and drawn.

Pume said, "All my little performers. I trust you are ready for Act Two? Come, come! Show a little interest at least if you cannot muster enthusiasm. *I want you all to smile!*"

They all did.

"Much better. Much. Now, I want you to stay in your quarters today, each of you, when you've finished eating. Except for you, York. You and I and Gordon will begin adding to Sensory Central's library today. You, Villane, are to be first."

Villane's hands formed into fists beneath the table.

Addressing York, Pume continued, "Villane doesn't seem entirely delighted with the honor, does he?"

York said nothing. He ate, feeling the food like clay in his mouth. He avoided looking at the others.

Pume rose. "Finish, please." His tone was no longer bantering, no longer falsely jovial. "Back to your quarters. Villane, we shall be with you in just a moment."

They were. York arrived with Pume not far behind. Pume ordered Villane to lie down on his bed and Villane obeyed, watching York as he approached carrying the recordeck and wincing as its wires were fastened to his body. He felt nothing for a long moment and then York flicked a lever and he felt so many things so suddenly . . .

. . . *the floor is filthy and there are rats. In the corner there. Eyes, red. This prison is a stinking pile of stones. I only stole a loaf. A single loaf. One!*

Then, York's distant voice, like a cry on the wind, "Can you smell anything?"

Rancid sweat and sour soup with things floating in it. Ruth!

"Let him go on," Pume instructed York, sensing the shift in Villane's imagery. "The Priestmen can edit later."

Don't shut the damned door! Ruth, let me in! I need—

"What's happening now, Villane?" York questioned, watching the spool spin in the recordeck.

The door. Pounding on the door. Knuckles hurt. Ruth!

The session lasted for nearly an hour during which York or Pume and sometimes both of them held bottles under Villane's nose filled with acrid or musky solutions of substances. They pinched portions of his flesh. They made sounds at the edges of his ears. They flashed light in his open eyes, showed him colors, as the recordeck ate it all. When it was over, York switched off the recordeck which Pume picked up and carried away and with it, pieces of Villane—his pain, his singing joy, his entire captured cataract of sensations and feelings that had once been his alone.

In Sensory Central that same afternoon, the program from the recordeck was delivered to the Priestman in charge. He took it from the messenger Pume had sent and carried it with him into the editing room. There he handed it to one of the other Priestmen present and told them what it was. "Specimen Phillip Villane. One of our Supreme Priestman's prime sources of material at present," he elaborated. "This one will have to be edited and then properly filed. See what it has to offer."

The Priestmen turned on the reelback unit. Needles leaped on dials and wires flamed with incandescence as the spool unwound. The Priestmen heard Villane scream in their headsets and they quickly checked intensity levels. They saw, on the screen above their heads, the dimensional translate of Villane's passion. It glowed with crimson life, faded and sprang again into a yellow joy as naked bodies, Villane's and a woman's, gyrated in what looked at first like a clumsy battle but was nothing more nor less than the choreography of love. Abruptly, the picture changed. Villane sat alone in a dark prison cell. The dials registered his sense of its stench and the Priestmen were momentarily overwhelmed by the wave of hysterical fear that flowed through the circuits of the reelback.

"Neutralize the receptors," barked one of the Priestmen when the program finally came to an end. "What was the meaning of the prison scene? It did seem moral enough. But that other one, that one with the woman—?"

"Everything has its place, everything its time," quoted his superior. "Ours is not to reason why, ours is but to help minds fly."

"Correction noted and assimilated," said the first Priestman humbly.

"Then let's get on with it. I see from his file that the specimen's sense-set was based in part on the fact that the book he was assigned was about prison and crime. *Les Miserables*. We'll edit the tape into two separate units then. File the lusty one under Celebrations, the other under Miscellaneous. We'll be able to append additional appropriate material as it is submitted from other specimens to round the latter one out. It can be made suitable for some of the more euphoric citizens who come to us and who are in need, as we so well know, of some chastening."

As the editing proceeded, Villane's feelings became matters of some moment in the hands of the Priestmen as they dissected, spliced and occasionally intensified portions of what had once been the private products of Villane's mind and memory.

Outside in the reception room, the many people waited with varying degrees of patience for their turns.

An obese woman fidgeted in her chair and chattered to the man next to her. Her head habitually swiveled compulsively to the right in little uncontrolled jerks. She said, "They say the first time's always the best. This is my first time. You been here before?"

"I been," the man answered.

"What's it like? Tell me what it's like."

"Well," the man drawled, wishing this woman would go away or at least stop jerking her head in such a sinister fashion. "Well," he went on, "it's never twice the same, you know. They take you in and they talk things over with you a little."

"What do they say? What do they want to know?"

"Oh, just about your job, what it is. How you like it. What seems to be your problem. They're really very nice."

"Oh, I'm glad. To tell you the truth," she whispered conspiratorially, her head rapidly jerking, "I'm just a little bit scared. But I said to my husband, Jack, I said, I got to go down to Sensory Central or I'll go clean out of my mind. Jack, he just laughed and told me to go ahead and do what I wanted. I'm under contract to the Nursery, you know, and it's driving me wild!"

Her listener nodded.

Undaunted by his lack of response, the woman rambled on, "Jack—he's my husband, did I tell you? Anyway, Jack he's not getting any younger and he's always tired and like that. I'm a very emotional type person. Do you think they'll understand?"

"I'm sure they will. Oh, see, they're ready for you."

A Priestman stood in the doorway and beckoned to the fat woman.

Her head jerking more violently than ever, she rose and followed him into the pool of violet light that bathed the Interview Section.

Once inside and seated across from him, she heard him say in a lukewarm voice, "No need to fear, dear lady. Now, why don't you tell me why you're here." He crossed his legs and his robe swirled about his boots that caught and reflected the violet glow of the light.

"Why, to relax, I guess," the woman declared.

The Priestman nodded his encouragement, clasping his hands together.

The woman told him about Jack getting older. She described the long lonely nights. She cried a little. The

Priestman handed her a facecloth and then he led her into one of the little cubicles and helped her make herself comfortable on one of the pallets. "We will fill your heart and head to help you carry on," he told her, as he scraped some skin from her fingers and fastened the electrolytic pins in her flesh.

"Ooohhh!" she exclaimed. "That stings!"

"Not for long. Not for long. Please be patient." He inserted the spool he had selected for her in the side of the pallet and told her to relax. He connected the terminals and left the room and the woman who was already sighing in the arms of a young man who did not look at all like her husband.

Silently, the spool spun.

It was over too soon to suit the woman. She groaned as the Priestman, bending over her, removed the pins and handed her first a facecloth to wipe the perspiration from her body and then ointment to ease the tingling sensation that remained in her flesh where the pins had been.

"Is that all?" she whimpered. "It was just getting good."

"Quite all," the Priestman told her. "Now, we must have our little exit chat."

She blundered her way out of the pallet and followed him. Her head no longer jerked. She moved more slowly. Her eyes were calm although in them disappointment at the brevity of the experience did battle with the glow of contentment that still lingered in her huge body.

"I see by your records," said the Priestman, as they sat in the Interview Section once more, "that you have helped deliver eleven percent more Limbos than is required under your contract."

Proudly, the woman said, "I'm a hard worker."

"And you'll work even harder now," commented the Priestman cryptically.

"I'm not sure I get you."

He said, "Would you like to come back to us some day soon?"

A gift worthy of kings! "Oh, yes!" the woman exclaimed. "I sure would."

"You can."

"Thank you. You're kind."

"You can," the Priestman repeated, "just as soon as your quota excess reaches sixteen percent."

The woman gasped. "Sixteen percent? But I work harder than most as it is. You said so yourself! You said—"

The Priestman stood up. "Sixteen percent, dear lady. Save Cityside!"

The woman let herself be ushered out of the Interview Section. As she boarded the carveyor, she decided it had been worth it. No doubt about that. But sixteen percent! The man who was a myth floated back behind her eyes. Sixteen percent it would have to be she told him and herself. Because she sure did intend to come back!

With each week that passed, Cityside's citizens fed on the programs extracted almost hourly from Pume's flock of minds imprisoned in his apartment. The Priestmen told the people that they saw Cityside and its citizens flourishing and what they saw was good. Sensory Central was at last forced, because of a stampeding attendance rate, to remain open twenty-four hours a day. It sat like an active hive in the center of Cityside, while inside it the people lay dreaming on their pallets like briefly hibernating animals.

But they were all active in their fashion. On the lenses of their minds gladiators sprang and feinted and the smell of blood mixed with the sand beneath their feet startled their nostrils and injured their eyes. They heard lions roar their husky challenges and saw monkeys dart through the skyscape of the treetops. They felt fear prowl in hidden alleys where the light never ventured as Jack the Ripper's scalpel slit the night and throat of the painted girl who had smiled at him. They heard the singing whips descend on flinching flesh and they watched the oars of the galleys dip and rise, dip and rise like manic dolphins. They smelled roses in a summer garden and cooling apple pies steaming on window sills under the watchful eyes of robins. These and more scenes and sensations flowed through the twisting minds of the people as they slid deeper into their brief reality that was as slick as slanting rain and seeded their brains with wonder.

But there was always an ending and a rising up of the people from their pallets and a going away from Sensory Central after the exit interviews during which they were admonished to work hard because work wins. The Priestmen spoke to the people of percentages and performance improvement and the people listened and bowed their heads as the Priestmen punched their identicards and returned them to their slots in the memory banks.

At times, there were scenes. Scenes made by people returning hungrily to Sensory Central and being coldly told by the Priestmen that no, the figures on the identicards did not lie. Their production was down. But there was always tomorrow and the day after that. Sometimes the people fled down the halls in desperation and tried to force their way into the cubicles and were pulled back and dragged away past the others waiting hopefully in the Reception Room and thrown down the stairs into the street. The Priestmen sincerely regretted such incidents. They told the people so as they lay wailing on the steps and pleading for just one more time and whispering slyly that they would pay. But it was all useless. There were the facts and there were the figures on the identicards and the people soon learned that no subterfuge worked. Implacable were the Priestmen.

So the people picked themselves up and went home. They wept. They cursed. Invitably, they faced the cold fact that they could return to Sensory Central at any time —at any time after they had met their quotas.

Many girls volunteered their services as Breedettes. When they were accepted, their indenticards were properly coded. The Life Laboratory began to hum with increased activity. In the Nursery, there was a long waiting list in the contract file and many women were roughly turned away who wanted to help deliver and nurse the Limbos. People sat up nights and pounded their foreheads as they tried to think of new and ingenious ways of serving Cityside. The more imaginative among them succeeded. One bright day, an idea was presented in eloquent terms concerning the possibility of using certain less efficient members of the community as decoys to lure Landsenders close enough to Limboland so that the Limbos could then seize and kill them. The originator of the idea, a boy of fourteen, was given free access to Sensory Central for life. And he went there gladly, sometimes more than once a day, not knowing that what he was seeking was his own temporary death while his proud parents talked about him and his imagination to their admiring friends.

The world turned on its axis and everyone smiled. Over their culture trays and their assembly lines where they fused the splinter bombs, they smiled and smiled at each other, telling themselves and each other that the Priestmen were right. *The best is.* Sensory Central was always there, waiting for them. And when the long days ended and night came trooping through the streets, the people did not speak because they were busy remembering the monkeys they had seen careening through the treetops and the secret unnamed men and women who had lulled them to delicious sleep beside shimmering lakes or taken their hands and walked with them in silent communication through meadows where flowers filled the air with their sultry perfume.

When the first person accused them of having cheated him, the Priestmen showed no rage but hustled him away to the Interrogation Vault and placed him in one of the deep pits and asked him many probing questions. When he maintained his heretical charge, they sent him to the Disposal Depot, still screaming wild accusations. There hoses were turned on him until he eventually quieted. But it was not the hoses that had silenced him. It was instead the stopping of his pounding heart.

All went well for a time. The Priestmen stacked their

spools—the ones Pume provided regularly—higher and higher. They installed seven hundred additional cubicles.

Then the second person, a girl this time, made the same charge as had the man earlier. Hesitantly, she asked a question during her exit interview. "Do you think maybe there's something wrong with me? I could hardly feel *anything*."

The Priestmen sent her away and went at once to consult their superiors. They checked the spool the girl had been experiencing. They put it on the reelback, inserted the pins in their own flesh and felt the soft grass under their bare feet and then the tingling of their skin as they swam, full of frolic, in the mountain lake. It was all there. They had felt it. Perhaps, they speculated, there had indeed been something wrong with the girl. They summoned her the next day and gave her a second, different spool. Again, when it ended, the girl admitted that she had felt nothing. Alarm rang in her eyes.

They checked her records carefully. She was one of the volunteer breedettes. She had been to Sensory Central thirteen times, they discovered. "At first," she explained to the Priestman questioning her, "it was okay. Why, I could hardly stand up after! But then it got so it wasn't the same anymore. Like I told you, I can't feel hardly anything now."

The Priestmen reached a conclusion which they soon found to be a correct one. The degree of sensory reaction, they decided, diminished in direct correlation with the number of visits a person had made to Sensory Central. Clearly, something would have to be done. The matter was aggravated as more and more people began to complain that they felt little or nothing during their sessions.

The Priestmen promptly closed Sensory Central for a indefinite time. This proved to be a serious mistake. A riot took place in front of its doors. People screamed to be admitted. People fell to their knees and begged for mercy. Breasts were beaten as eyes rolled insanely in their sockets. A contingent of Priestmen at last came out from behind the locked doors and, wielding thick clubs, beat the people back. They kicked and they clubbed but they never stopped, during all of this, their chanting. "The best is! Everything always turns out for the best!"

When the streets were empty again, the Priestmen met together and worked around the clock. Each spool in the library was placed on the reelback and its parameters altered and its sense-set intensified. New electrolytic pins were quickly manufactured which were designed to go deeper into the flesh of the people and a way was found to measure the static electricity of a person's brain and body and, if it was discovered to be too low, it could be increased to allow fuller receptivity through the new, deeper implants.

At last, over a week since Sensory Central had been hastily closed, it opened again. The people flocked in as if to a festival. They grinned obsequiously at the Priestmen and at each other and some of the children became so excited at the prospect of what lay ahead that they had to be forcibly restrained by a specially trained group of Priestmen using little whips.

Crisis gave way to spectacular success. Even those who had been to Sensory Central as many as twenty times left dazed—stunned by their new and deepr sensations and delights.

The Priestmen accepted the murmured gratitude of the people and their shouted adulation and said meekly in reply, "Do unto Landsenders what Landsenders want to do to you."

"Save Cityside!" cried the people and they went back to their work with a renewed sense of purpose.

Pume was furious and he made no effor to disguise the fact. He raged through the apartment, yelling for Gordon to come and help him and smashing his fist into the palm of his hand. "She'll do as I say or I'll blast her skull to shreds!"

Gordon galloped in and Pume yelled at him, "Where's Cameron?"

"Don't know," came Gordon's thought.

"Find her! Bring her here!"

Not waiting for Gordon, Pume hurried down the hall and tried Ruth's door. Locked. He pounded his thick fists on it and shouted to her to come out. That very morning he had told her that she and Villane were to be linked for a special session with the recordeck and she had stared at him in disbelief and run from the room. He had thought nothing of it at the time but now that he was ready to begin she was nowhere to be found. He stopped his pounding, his fury momentarily succumbing to a sudden flash of reason. He fumbled in his pocket and withdrew the key to Ruth's room. With his lips a thick crease in the flesh of his face, he turned the key and flung back the door. The room was empty.

Gordon arrived and grabbed Pume's hand. Pume turned, ready to strike blindly, until he saw who it was. "What? The laboratory?"

Gordon began pulling him in that direction. Marveling, as he always did at moments like this, at Gordon's strength, Pume let himself be led to the laboratory. Gordon threw open the door and flung out an arm at the end of which his pointing finger flickered like a beacon. Pume looked in the direction Gordon had indicated and saw only the wheeled table and the white sheet covering it and reaching all the way to the floor.

"Beneath!" It was Gordon sending again.

Pume strode to the table and ripped the sheet from it, sending a pillow flying to the floor. Cowering under the table, he discovered Ruth. He felt like seizing her and shaking her and striking her until the blood flowed and she screamed for forgiveness. Instead, he visibly relaxed and said, "Come out, Cameron. At once. I am not a patient man."

Ruth crawled out from under the table and stood up. Only fear could be found in her once proud face.

"I told you to be ready, Cameron. But you prefer this hide-and-find, I see. Well, I've found you, haven't I?" Pume punctuated his words with a slap that turned Ruth's cheek crimson.

She remained rigid, stifling the impulse to raise her hand to the flaming area of her face.

"Come," Pume commanded, turning. He reached the door and looked back. Ruth remained standing beside the table. "Gordon!" he snapped.

The dwarf had been waiting for this moment. He raced to Ruth and threw his small arms around her knees. Like a slender tower, she fell in a heap. Gordon hopped about her, his little feet kicking and his fists pummeling her as Pume watched.

Ruth's cries echoed in the room and snaked out into the corridor. Hearing them, Villane came running. He collided with Pume and then recoiled from the sight of Gordon striking Ruth again and again. "Stop it!" he shouted, and lunged for Gordon. Seeing this new victim, Gordon adroitly darted aside and Villane fell on Ruth, striking his head against the leg of the table which went rolling across the room as a result of the impact.

Pume laughed as he reached for the box at his breast. He pressed Villane's button and heard him scream. He motioned to Gordon. Gordon grabbed Ruth's hair and began to drag her from the room. Her hands flew up to claw at his fingers but he did not flinch or release her. Pume stepped aside as he dragged her, moaning, from the laboratory.

Pume released his finger that had been pressing the button on his box. "Villane," he said, "you are no hero. When will you learn?"

Villane rolled on the floor, awash in a pool of pain and he shouted obscenities at Pume who only smiled and beckoned to him, indicating that he was to come along. Helplessly, Villane staggered to his feet and followed Pume down the hall to Ruth's room. They entered to find Gordon strapping Ruth to the bed. He had pasted adhesive over her mouth and in so doing had carelessly imprisoned strands of her hair beneath the white patch. He tore the hair loose and it came away in his fingers. Ruth groaned and writhed as tears dripped from her eyes that were wide with fear.

Docile, Villane took his place on the bed Gordon rolled in and positioned next to Ruth's. Pume pressed another button and soon York appeared in the doorway, carrying the rocordeck. Villane saw at once that York was stunningly drunk. He could barely stand. The recordeck wobbled in his hands and he seemed oblivious of Pume's flaming eyes upon him. When he did at last notice them, he grinned a lopsided grin and said, "Dontcha worry. Practice makes perfect. I can do it."

He did. He wired Ruth first. Then Villane who watched his twitching mouth and found himself, with great surprise, pitying this giant of a man so sick with disaster.

Villane felt himself drift away as the recordeck hummed and soon he was lost in a warm rich coil of love that wound around him and he imagined that he took Ruth's head in his hands and kissed her mouth and told her that there was an end to pain. Then everything faded again and he felt her body through her thin dress. Then they were skipping up a mountain, laughing, and the world was wonderful and sweet . . .

"Now for Sister," Pume said, when the two bodies on the beds were motionless at last.

"Shishter," York repeated dully.

She shrank back against the wall of the room as they entered. Her eyes darted like fawns at the sound of a crashing cougar from one to the other of the figures facing her.

"Do you have to?" she cried. "Didn't you get enough last time?"

"Silence!" Pume bellowed. He had had about enough for one day. He gestured impatiently at York. "Get on with it!"

When Sister was transfixed on her bed with open, unseeing eyes and connected to the recordeck in her room, they left, Gordon hurrying down the hall ahead of them to Grandsir's room.

Grandsir gave them no trouble, only looked up, put

down his book, got into bed and flung out his arms wearily as if to a too familiar lover.

Later, Pume and York sat alone in the living room, conscious of the faint moans and occasional brisk cries emanating from the individual rooms beyond. "You're not to drink anymore, York," Pume said. "You need a clear head for this business."

"Need to," murmured York.

"Your needs are of no moment to me, York. They are, I think I should remind you, determined only by my desires."

York shook his head as if to rid his brain of the noise of Pume.

They sat in silence for some time, a silence which was finally broken by the tocking of the factclock on the wall:

Any citizen knowing of weak or traitorous thoughts or behavior on the part of any other citizen is ordered to report same at once to the nearest Priestman. Reward: Sensory Central Resident Status. Time Four-o-six. Work hard. Work wins.

York swore drunkenly.

Pume rose and headed for the door. "Come on, York. They must be depleted by now. The spools are probably full."

York raised himself up with effort and swayed down the hall after Pume. He disconnected Grandsir and then Sister, leaving them to awaken by themselves. It took him longer to remove the wires from Villane and Ruth because of the more intricate network of complicated neuron connectors.

When he was finished, York took the spools and once again followed Pume as he left to find the reelback unit to see what they had gotten this time.

Villane was the first to recover. Shakily, he swung his legs over the side of the bed and went to where Ruth lay, her eyelids fluttering. "Ruth," he whispered.

She opened her eyes dreamily. She sat up, her face flushing.

Villane said, "I'm sorry about what just happened. I'm really sorrier than you know."

Ruth felt a kindred sorrow but she did not say so. She found herself wondering what love was like when it was real and not merely a commodity. As she thought about it, she began to ask herself questions. If the thoughts were there and if the feelings came during these sessions, well, then, was it not true that what she felt was indeed real, however unexpressed previously? Slowly, the blood drained from her face and she began to realize the truth of what, until now, she had believed was only fantasy, falsity. She took Villane's hand in her own and drew him to her. His hand was cold in hers. "Are you really sorry?" she asked him.

"Yes," he said.

"For wanting me?"

"No!" he protested. "No, I mean, I'm sorry for embarrassing you."

"Phillip, look at me please."

He did. Her radiant eyes warmed him and now it was his face that flushed.

"Phillip," she continued, "there's no need to be sorry. It's strange in a way. Now, I'm embarrassed to find that I was embarrassed when our minds met and we found that we—we wanted each other. That's good."

Villane began to understand. He began to see that what had caused him pain was something that should have brought him joy. If he were honest with himself and with Ruth and stopped playing games and ended the silly emotional editing he and, he supposed, everyone else had always practiced all their weary lives, all might yet be well. "I'm glad you're not sorry. I wish it didn't have to be like this though."

"Pume, you mean?"

"Yes," he said. "Our love is his merchandise now."

"But still ours!" she insisted. "Let it be on the spools! That doesn't mean that *we* don't still feel it."

He sank down on his knees before her, laying his head in her lap. He threw his arms around her and told the wealth of her body everything that was on the spool and still in his heart. She listened happily and when he had finished she said, "Lie own. Here, with me. No, never mind about the door. Our private feelings are public property already. If anyone sees, they will be seeing nothing they could not see and hear and feel themselves because of Pume and his grand larceny."

Sister passed the open door and looked in. She stood there for a moment and something inside her cried out for something that had no name for her as yet but left her feeling bereft, feeling that she had already lost something precious that she had never really owned.

She went on down the hall, deliberately emptying her mind. But her mind would not stay empty. She found herself thinking of other places. The Dump. The streets down below. Other people. The vague image of the sharp-faced woman who had been her mother. The almost transparent man who had called her, if she remembered correctly, "Bad thing." *Bad thing.* I can't help it if I can teleport, she thought. She thought about going away. Down on the streets. It would be so simple. Think *there* and *there* I am, she told herself. But she knew it wouldn't work. Pume would press her little button and she'd have to come back. She gritted her teeth and turned to enter the living room. She paused as the voices drifted out to her. It was Pume speaking. She listened, flattening herself against the wall.

"Not a thing worth saving!"

Then, York's voice. "Editing might help. Maybe the Priestmen could sharpen the focus."

"No," Pume declared emphatically. "Sister's spool is an utter waste. All we got—you heard it for yourself—were simpering cries for someone she can't even project clearly. That and infantile fantasies of killing and swallowing people alive. No one wants to feel things like that at Sensory Central. No, York, I'm afraid it's no use bothering with Sister anymore."

Outside the room, Sister grew cold. Was she good for nothing at all, she wondered.

"Give her a book to read," York pleaded. "Something simple. The kid's got imagination, I'm certain of it. She ought to be able to come up with something then."

"You're forgetting," Pume said, "that Sister's never been in the study cribs. She can't even read!"

Sister fled down the hall, afraid to listen any longer. She threw open the door of Grandsir's room and was about to cry out to him when she saw that he was sleeping. She wanted to wake him. She moved toward his lean figure in the bed. He stirred but did not waken. "Grandsir," she said too softly for him to hear. "It's Sister. Oh, Grandsir, something awful is going to happen. I know it. They say I don't know anything or not enough or something." She knelt down beside the bed. "But," she told the sleeping Grandsir, "I can teleport. That's something. I could get away." No sooner were the words spoken, than she knew that everything was hopeless. She stood up, straightened her blouse and smoothed her skirt, and touched the shoulder of the old man. "Take care of yourself, Grandsir," she said. "If anything happens to me, I mean, who'll look after you then?"

Grandsir stirred under her gentle touch and she quickly withdrew her hand. Then she turned and quietly left the room, closing the door behind her. In the hall again, she did not know where to go. She did not want to go back to the living room where Pume and York were probably still talking terrible things. Or to Ruth and Villane, not now. She went to her own room and sat down in front of her little mirror and looked at the girl imprisoned in it. The two girls shook their heads and wiped their eyes. "I don't care!" one said. And the other girl in the mirror mouthed it but without conviction.

Villane left Ruth after making her promise to trust him and after telling her that he would somehow find a way out for all of them from the cages in which Pume kept them caught. He went in search of York with only the vaguest notion of what he was going to do but the clearest realization that something must be done if they were to retain not only their sanity but their very identities. He found York sitting alone in the living room, still drunk and only partly awake.

Villane went to him and shook his shoulder. "York, wake up! I want to talk to you."

"Who's it?" York stammered, raising his hams of hands as if in self-defense.

"It's Villane. Wake up, man!"

"I'm sick," York sighed, peering at Villane through reddened eyes.

Villane hauled him to his feet, staggering under the weight of York's great body, and managed to get him into the cleanroom where he held him under the sanispray. York emerged dripping several minutes later. He looked down at himself, at his wet clothes, and then gestured helplessly at Villane with outspread palms.

"I'll get you something dry to put on," Villane said.

Later, when York had changed and they were seated in Villane's quarters, Villane found that he did not really know how to say what he wanted to say. And he realized that that was due to the simple fact that he did not *know* what precisely it was that he wanted to say. Clearing his throat, he made a stab at it. "York, we've got to get out of here. As soon as possible.

"You must be crazy, Villane."

"I don't think I am. But I think I will be—all of us will be—if we don't do something, and soon, to save ourselves."

"I knew you for a hero the minute I met you," York mocked.

"Cut it out," Villane snapped. "Listen to me. Help me. We've got to think of some way of getting out of here. Any ideas?"

"Lots. Number one, let's just walk out. Number two, let's kill Pume and take control of the Priestmen and run Cityside ourselves. Number three— Shall I go on?"

Villane's feeling of futility returned to smother him. He

thought back to another time. The time in the Life Laboratory when he had stood up and said to himself that he would not go to contributing to the black and dusty god of death that seemed enshrined in Cityside's womb and brain. What had become of that man he had been, that man who, though afraid, had taken the first vital step toward the sunlight of reason, the man who had said "no"? Well, things had happened since then, Villane reminded himself. One of those things was recorded for anyone to see in the skull of the no-sayer—the small metal sound disk. But, Villane argued with himself, could he let pain be his master and fear his only king? The problem resolved itself once again into the same issue he had confronted earlier. He would simply have to choose again and then be prepared to take the consequences of that choice.

"What are you thinking about, Villane?" York asked.

"I'm trying to remember what it's like to be a man."

"Is your memory working?"

"Yes, it is. York, consider this. Surgery put these receivers in our heads so surgery ought to be able to take them out. Maybe we could force Gordon to—"

York's laughter drowned Villane's words. "No one forces Gordon to do anything. Give it up, Villane. It's hopeless. We are too."

"Maybe you are, York. But I'm not. Not quite yet. I'll think of something. Go back to your bottle!"

York watched him leave the room and he did not blame him for his sarcasm. Villane, after all, was young and he probably still believed that Death's long list omitted his name. He had not yet discovered the true length and all-inclusive nature of the list but, York knew, he would and then he would look more carefully ahead of him before putting one foot in front of the other. He would learn the bitter truth—that survival was often built upon a shaky collection of compromises. York got up and went to the serviset. He was about to dial a drink when Pume came into the room.

"No more libations, York. There's work to do."

"Sister?" York asked, afraid of the answer he nevertheless expected.

"Yes. I'm sending her back to the Disposal Depot. I'm convinced she is of no further value to me. Gordon's searching for her now. I want you to help keep her calm. I haven't told the others. Grandsir would only hinder us because of his concern for the child. It may be necessary to trap her. We might have to use force. York, stand over there by the door."

York hesitated briefly as his mind made ready to embrace still one more compromise. He moved slowly toward the door.

Gordon appeared in the room, his mind reaching out to Pume's. *"She's coming! She's coming!"*

Pume took a glass of chocolate milk from the serviset and sprinkled a powder into it. "This will put her out long enough to get her to the Depot. Gordon, if there's trouble, keep the others out of here."

Across the room, the words crashed in York's ears. *The others.* Was he then, on Pume's side? He forced himself to smile as Sister stepped warily into the room. His smile withered as he saw her staighten and toss her head in curt defiance. He guessed what the effort at pretense was costing her.

"Sister, I want to talk to you," Pume said. "Come and sit here by me."

Sister gazed at Pume through slightly narrowed eyes. "What do you want to talk about? What's *he* doing over there?"

York said, "I'm just hanging around. Nothing better to do."

Sister was obviously unsatisfied with York's explanation. She glanced nervously over her shoulder and then at Pume.

"Your favorite," he said, holding out the glass of chocolate milk to her.

"I don't want it."

Pume made an effort to maintain his self-control, thinking that a little sound shock might be warranted after all. "Drink it!" he commanded. He stood up and thrust the glass at Sister.

York moved forward swiftly and knocked the glass from Pume's hand as if by accident. "Oh, sorry," he apologized. "Awfully clumsy of me. I meant to hand it to her. Wait, I'll dial another."

Sister peered at York. She thought she had read something in his glance. As the floor vents cleaned the mess at her feet, Sister spoke to Pume. "What do you want to talk to me about?"

"Never mind!" Pume snapped as he leaned forward to seize her.

Sister vanished.

"York!" Pume yelled, "you damned idiot! Now she's gone! I'll deal with you later, you can be sure of that. Now, after her!"

York remained motionless. Thinking of Villane who was so young, he let himself hope that he was not yet too old to act in the face of necessity. The thought—the hope—gave him momentary ease. He hoped Sister was gone for good this time.

Pume, with Gordon's eager help, searched throughout the apartment. Sister was nowhere to be found. Pume repeatedly pressed her button on his little box to no avail. She did not reappear. He raced wildly to the visifone, pressed the floor pedal to turn it on and waited impatiently for the face of the Priestmen to appear on the screen. When it did, he barked, "One of my people has escaped—the child." He proceeded to describe Sister to the Priestman. "You'll be able to find her by her screaming if she hasn't gone too far," he added, grinning. The Priestman nodded. The visifone blanked. Pume left it and switched on the scanscreen. The streets of Cityside sprang into three dimensional life on it. Pume paced up and down in front of the scanscreen, compulsively pressing the tiny button and watching as the robed legions of Priestmen appeared and began scouring the streets and the buildings in search of Sister.

Sister did not know precisely where she was. It was very dark and she guessed that she was in the basement of one of Cityside's buildings because of the humming of dynamos in the distance and the faint clicking of invisible meters punctuating the darkness. She leaned down and pulled up her skirt. She ripped the strip of adhesive tape from her thigh to free the scapel she had stolen earlier from Gordon's equipment. She had planned to use it to kill Pume if he had touched her. Suddenly, she dropped the knife and began to wail as the receiver severed her thoughts with its fingers of pain. She fell sobbing to her knees, her fingers clawing desperately at the metal disk, struggling in vain to suppress her shrieks that bore loud testimony to the pain that was assaulting her.

Shuddering and still moaning as the pain momentarily lessened, she groped about in the darkness for the fallen scalpel. At last, she found it and raised it to her head. Her hand shook and her body trembled. She waited tensely. The pain returned in undulating waves, sharp, intense. Fading a little. Returning. Sister slid the scalpel into the flesh above her ear. She cried out in pain and more tears came. Her fingers groped and found hair and gore and, at last, purchase on the metal plate which she seized and ripped free, its tiny filaments bloodied. She fainted.

When she regained consciousness untold minutes later, it was still dark and the darkness seemed alive with the pain of her violated flesh. She raised her still sticky fingers and found that the blood had begun to clot. She was surprised that there seemed to be so little of it.

She crouched, barely breathing, in the darkness, moving her head gingerly, trying to determine which movements caused her pain and which did not.

Light suddenly flooded the room and Sister screamed as if struck. Blinded briefly, she clutched the scalpel in her hand expecting Pume to appear before her. She would kill him!

"Search and destroy!" came the cry from somewhere overhead.

Sister looked up to see several Priestman on the catwalk above her.

"There she is!" cried one of them, pointing down at her.

Summoning all her strength, Sister thought *away!*

She appeared in the middle of a mall filled with iron sculpture and searching Priestman. The blood began to flow again from her self-inflicted wound and dizziness gripped her. She wavered like wheat before the reaper and tried to run as the Priestmen raced down the ramp in her direction. She fell.

They stood over her, gazing down at her body sprawled against the concrete and they loudly rejoiced. They bent down and picked up her limp form and raised it high above their heads and marched in rigid formation out of the park and down the street in the direction of the Disposal Depot.

In Pume's apartment, Grandsir stared in shocked disbelief at the scanscreen, watching without wanting to, the tiny drops of blood dripping down from Sister's head onto the yellow robe of the Priestman in the rear as they carried her into the Disposal Depot and the great gate closed behind them.

He felt rage envelop him and he shook his head slowly from side to side as if trying to deny the truth of what he had just witnessed. His eyes closed and then opened again and he turned like a plaster figure in an ancient clock about to announce the weather, from Ruth to York and then to Villane.

Pume sighed and switched off the scanscreen. "Well, that's that!"

Grandsir, behind him, moved forward, his hand reaching out to pick up the thick book on the table at his side. He raised the book as Pume was about to turn and brought it down with a resounding thud on Pume's head. As if it were a signal, the others sprang to sudden life. Villane grabbed the book from Grandsir who was weeping soundlessly now and he struck Pume a second blow, causing bruises on his forehead to bloom into purple life and unconsciousness to come to him.

Ruth, her lips drawn tautly back over her teeth, ran to Pume and bent down over him. She tore open his robe and tugged at the straps that bound the box to his chest. "Help me, Phillip!" she cried.

Together, they unbuckled the straps and stood up, Ruth holding aloft the box like a trophy in her hand. Villane took it from her and flung it against the nearest wall. He went to it and, like an enraged beast, stamped it into a tangled mass of flashing silicon and colored wires and useless black buttons. Breathing heavily, he turned to see Gordon rushing toward him.

"Look out, Villane!" York shouted.

But Villane needed no warning. Feeling the blood flow like fire through his body giving him a new kind of strength, he tensed as Gordon leaped for his throat.

Villane staggered, gasping. Someone somewhere was shouting. Dimly, Villane recognized Ruth's voice. He tore at Gordon's fingers, drowning in the hate in Gordon's eyes so near his own, and succeeded in tearing loose first one hand and then the other. He threw Gordon to the floor and paused, his breath searing his lungs. Before he could move again, York leaped forward and grabbed Gordon by the ankles, lifted him up and swung him like an upside down doll, around and around and at last released him to fly through the air and crash against the far wall. From York's throat came a cry like that of a bull elephant in battle which slowly dissolved into a gusty sob as he stared at the broken body of the dwarf that lay gazing up lifelessly at nothing at all.

Ruth exclaimed, "Grandsir's gone!"

Villane looked about him. Grandsir was no longer in the room. "Maybe he's—"

"The Dump!" Ruth interrupted. "I'll bet he's gone to the Dump with some crazy idea of trying to save Sister!"

"Let's look around first," Villane said. "He might still be here somewhere."

"I'll take care of Pume," York said.

As Villane and Ruth left to search for Grandsir, York bent down over Pume's unconscious form. He reached up and ripped the cloth from the table, sending a vase filled with flowers clattering to the floor. He began to rip the tablecloth into slender strips. "Old fox," he murmured, "your chickens have rejected your roost. What will you do now? What good are you now, old fox, with no chickens left to terrorize?" Chuckling, he finished tying up Pume and then he rose and went to the corpse that had been Gordon. He lifted in in his arms and carried it to the window which he opened wide. He flung the body from him and leaned out to watch it fall like a tiny meteor through the sunny and artifically sweetened air.

Villane returned, followed by Ruth. "Grandsir's gone, all right," he announced. "What are you doing, York?"

York slammed the window shut and answered, "House cleaning."

Pume's pained groan startled them. "I'll call the Priestmen," he wheezed. "They'll get you!"

York walked over to where Pume lay. Touching him with his toe, he said, "You won't call anybody. You'll lie there and be quiet. The rest of us have matters to discuss and problems to solve."

Pume recoiled. He shut his mouth.

Villane said, "The first thing we've got to decide is what to do next. Ruth is convinced that Grandsir is headed for the Dump. She may be right. We could try to head him off. Even if he's not headed there, we can still have a go at trying to save Sister before she's sent into Landsend. Then, if we succeed, we can search for Grandsir later."

As they made their plans, talking in low voices, they failed to notice Pume slowly slide his corpulent body, inch by careful inch, toward the floor pedal that activated the visifone. His progress was agonizingly slow but it was progress nevertheless. At last he reached his goal and pressed his shoulder against the pedal. The visifone glowed into life. The face of a Priestman appeared on the screen. "Sir?"

"Help!" Pume yelled. "Get them!"

Villane and the others spun around as Pume shouted orders to the shocked Priestman who turned and bellowed to others off-screen. "Search and destroy! Save Supreme Priestman Pume!"

Villane sprang forward and dragged Pume's body away from the floor pedal. The screen went dark. "Damn you, Pume!" he exclaimed.

PART THREE

The Feat

VILLANE MARVELED at the joy he saw surging in Ruth's face and at York's low whistling as they made ready to leave Pume's apartment and go out into the streets of Cityside and the task that awaited them there. He marveled too at his own lack of fear, the fear that had crept along beside him for so long like a succubus keeping just out of sight but never out of mind.

He looked down at Pume where he lay still bound and silent now because of the strip of plaster he had placed across his mouth that locked his words away but not the hate darting like lances from his fat eyes.

Now that they were actually ready to depart, Villane hesitated. He thought it might be because the horror here was known. But out there in the streets what awaited them? He shook his head resolutely to free it from the swiling mist of indecision that threatened to engulf him and strode to the door where Ruth and York stood waiting for him.

"We'll head for the Dump," he said. "If we find Grandsir, we'll take him with us. You ready?"

Ruth answered, "Yes."

York nodded. "Even if we fail, we'll have made one helluva good try!"

Villane tossed him a grin and they left the apartment,

paying no attention to the sound of Pume's thrashing about on the floor as he sought desperately to free himself.

They dropped down in the tube and walked out beneath the sun smiling down at Cityside. Villane felt Ruth suddenly shrink back against him as a squad of Priestmen marched by in single file, their heads hidden beneath their cowls, their hands devoutly clasped around the guns they held ready in front of them.

Villane placed his arm around her and felt her relax. They stepped aboard the carveyor as it halted at the turntable switch.

An ice-eyed Priestman on his podium waved and the carveyor moved forward, gradually gaining momentum. Villane searched for Grandsir, his eyes roving from face to face among the people standing beside the buildings in little clusters and entering and leaving the shops. He was wondering what had possessed the old man, what had led him to do what he had done, an act so foolishly brave. He was intensely grateful for whatever it was because it had set in motion the creaking machinery of freedom, a freedom that he reluctantly admitted to himself might yet prove to be all too temporary.

York leaned toward Villane and whispered, "How does it feel to fly?"

Villane shot him a glance empty of comprehension. "Fly?"

"Flee, then. Fly. Be free. I feel drunker now than ever I did from the dubious products of Pume's serviset."

"Look!" Villane said suddenly. "Up ahead there!"

York looked and saw Grandsir.

Villane hastily pressed the signal button and the carveyor slowed, then stopped. They got off and started walking back to where Grandsir wandered bewildered. The book he carried was open and he kept turning its pages without ever looking at the pages he turned.

"He's dazed," Villane declared. "We'll have to take it easy with him."

"There aren't any Priestmen around," York said. "If

we have to, we can hustle him into one of the connecting Sector passages and try to talk to him there."

Ruth was the first to reach Grandsir. She planted herself in his path but he stepped around her without looking at her face and continued on his way, turning page after page of his unread book. "Grandsir," she softly called after him. "It's Ruth." She retraced her steps until she was beside him again. She reached out and took the book from his unprotesting hands. As she did so, he studied her quizzically.

Villane joined them, York a step behind. Ruth handed the book to York. "Get rid of it," she told him.

"Grandsir," Villane said quietly. "Are you all right?"

Grandsir looked at each of them without giving any sign of recognition. His hair drifted down around his wrinkled forehead like the ghost of a long ago snow. He said, "Has anyone seen her?"

"Sister?" Ruth asked.

Grandsir nodded.

"We're on our way to help her," Ruth told him. "If we can," she added.

"She never stays in one place for long, I know," Grandsir said. "But this time it's different somehow."

Ruth guided Grandsir toward the entrance to one of the Sector connections and when they were in the well-lighted and momentarily empty tunnel, she halted, her hand firmly gripping his thin arm.

Villane stepped forward and said, "Harsh measures are called for, I think." He raised his hand and brought it down with a resounding slap against the old man's face. *"Grandsir!"*

Like a sleeper waking, Grandsir whirled up from the chasm of his lost thoughts and staggered slightly. Villane shoved him back against the wall so that he would not fall.

"I—" Grandsir mumbled. "You—" Then he fell forward against Villane who held him close while his world shifted sharply and he gradually returned, piece by tortured piece, from the painful journey he had been on.

"Villane," York cautioned, "this is no good. Someone might come."

Villane took Grandsir's shoulders in his hands and held him away from his own body, looking into his face. "You're fine now. You're okay."

"Villane, did you see?" Grandsir moaned. "Did you see what they did to her?"

"We saw," Villane acknowledged. "We're going to try to save her."

The four of them moved out of the passage and began to walk in the direction of the Depot. As they walked, they discussed possible plans.

Villane proposed that they simply ask for admittance to the Dump. Declare themselves psych-sick, act the part. Ruth thought that they might try to disarm the Priestman on guard and force their way inside. Grandsir said that he didn't care how they got in but he was determined that they would get in. Sister was in there, he reminded them unnecessarily, and frightful things might be happening to her.

They did not realize how far or how fast they had walked until, turning a corner, they found themselves confronting the great gate of the Depot looming only yards away.

"I have an idea," York said. "Listen." He described the plan that had been born in his brain only a moment earlier. It was risky. It was wild. They decided to try it since no one had a better idea. York's plan represented the extent of their collective inventiveness.

Villane waited with Ruth and Grandsir as York walked toward the Priestman guarding the gate. When he was halfway there, he stopped, threw back his head and howled loudly. Like a sick wolf, he speared the dome overhead with his melancholy cries. The Priestman snapped alert and raised his airtube, inserting a tranquilagent as he did so. York began to run in eccentric circles. The Priestman, his face impassive, left his post and moved warily toward York. But York was here and there and everywhere all at once. The Priestman stalked him, his

123

airtube only inches from his lips and Villane saw with mounting delight that the first part of York's plan seemed to be working well. His seemingly senseless circling was leading the Priestman farther and farther away from the gate of the Depot.

Villane whispered, *"Now!"*

He ran to the gate, followed by Ruth and Grandsir, watched by the crowd of people who had gathered to see this curious game taking place before their vaguely interested eyes, its players York and the Priestman. Villane reached the gate first and ran his hands over the panel in its meshwork, pressing buttons, pulling levers in frantic and blind haste. At last, the gate swung slowly open. "York!" he shouted. "Come on!"

York stopped his howling when he heard Villane's shout and turned on the Priestman only steps away from him. He raised his huge fists and brought them down on the Priestman's head. The Priestman crumpled and fell, face down on the street, as the people gasped. No one moved to help York's victim. No one lifted a hand or a voice to help him. The people simply stood stunned as York bounced toward Villane and the open gate.

Together, they all ran inside and together they slammed the gate shut and stood panting in the reception room.

Villane caught his breath and whispered, "Through here."

They raced to the door at the far end of the room, opened it, entered and collided with two startled Priestmen.

Ruth moaned. Villane reached out for one of the Priestmen but the man dodged. "Stand, psych!" he bellowed hearshly.

Villane swung a fist. The Priestman seized it and expertly threw Villane to the floor. As York came running toward them, the Priestmen raised their clubs and struck, sending him flying across the room. Ruth shrank into the corner. Grandsir stepped in front of her. Villane tried to rise, found it impossible and slumped down again on the floor, helpless, as the flashing boot of the Priestman careened toward his head.

"Get them inside," the Priestman ordered his companion.

They forced Ruth and Grandsir to walk in front of them after summoning reinforcements to drag the unconscious bodies of Villane and York into the main arena where they were left, still unconscious, with Ruth and Grandsir bending over them, amid the shrieks and shouts of the psychs muddling about them. There was no sign of Sister anywhere.

Ruth knelt and placed Villane's head in her lap and wreathed it with her trembling fingers. Moments later, Villane's eyes burst open, their pupils flashing as he tried to raise his head. "Phillip," Ruth whispered, and the word was lost in the cacophony that dinned in the air of the Dump.

"Ruth," Villane said, struggling to rise. "Are you all right?"

She nodded and managed a slow smile. Villane stood up and helped her to her feet. He looked around the great arena, down at York who was conscious now and at Grandsir who seemed to have retreated again into some safer place inside himself, some more secure and tolerable harbor.

"So we're back again," Villane declared quietly, bitterly. "The circle is the perfect geometric figure. No beginning, no end. Start anywhere and end nowhere."

Ruth took him in her arms as she calibrated with fine and sensitive instruments of imagination that other private and infinitely complex geometry of her own heart. She found it strange—strange and oddly wonderful—that the love she felt flowering in her blood and brain could bloom here amidst the unweeded garden that was the Dump. But bloom it did and Villane's sturdy arms and his heart that she could feel beating beneath the all too vulnerable membrane of his skin reassured her and it did not seem to her at all frightful or alarming to find herself growing with him in this bizarre garden all gone to dry and dusty seed.

"Let's move over there," York suggested, gesturing toward a relatively unoccupied corner of the arena.

They followed him as he burrowed through the flux of bodies. Ruth looked back over her shoulder and saw Grandsir standing alone and seemingly unaware of their departure. She hurried back and took him by the hand. Docile, he let her steer him through the mob.

When they reached the corner York had designated, Ruth forced Grandsir to sit down on the floor. She crouched beside him, still holding his hand and hoping that she was protecting him but knowing that he had found his own protection in the maze of his dazed and withdrawn mind.

Villane and York stood over them, like shepherds conscientiously guarding the last remaining remnants of a decimated flock.

The noise in the arena washed against them, ebbing and flowing, like an immense tidal wave. The smell of urine and unwashed bodies assaulted their nostrils and their eyes registered shock as the psychs billowed like sheets in a wild wind about and around them. In their turrets high above it all, the Priestmen stared down impassively and without compassion or sympathy on these tattered threads that had once been part of the precisely patterned fabric of Cityside.

"Well, we got in," York commented. "I wish I had a drink."

"Sister must be here somewhere," Villane said. "Ruth, can you see her anywhere?"

Grandsir, hearing Sister named, returned to the here and now. He said, "I remember something Pume said. It was when you first came, Villane. He said something about Sister being drugged, I think, when they had her in the Dump before. So she couldn't teleport out. Maybe they've got her that way again. Maybe they've got her someplace separate. I'll go look."

"No, Grandsir," Villane said sharply. "You stay here.

I'll take a look around. The three of you stay here together so I'll be able to find you again."

"But—!" Grandsir protested.

"He's right," Ruth said, still holding Grandsir's hand and feeling uncomfortably like a little girl trying to play parent and not quite believing in the reality of the role. "Let Phillip search." She turned to Villane and whispered. "Be careful. Some of these people might be dangerous. And there are the Priestmen up there," she added, her gaze rising to the turrets, those efficient little castles haunted by unfeeling ghosts.

"I'll be all right," Villane assured her. He hoped he would be. He leaned toward Ruth and kissed her lightly on the lips, surprising her and himself as well. He moved cautiously out into the melee of the arena.

Ruth watched him go and Grandsir murmured something unintelligible as the pressure of her hand on his increased. York yearned for something that had no name and felt the fluttering in his stomach that was not caused by hunger alone.

Villane traced a path through the arena, guiding himself by the landmarks of the turrets. He noted the location of Ruth and the others in relation to the first turret above him and began to circle to the left, keeping the wall between himself and the psychs milling about or merely sitting idly, staring. It was impossible to tell where the doors were in the smooth wall. There were no cracks or discernible interstices. As he moved gingerly along the wall, touching it as if for support with the tips of his fingers, he began to count his steps in an effort to keep from thinking the thoughts that beat at his brain like savage birds. Maybe Sister had already been driven out into Landsend. *One, two, three, four—* She might be dead; her wound had been bleeding profusely. *Eleven, twelve—* The Priestmen killed as easily as they breathed. *Twenty-four, twenty-five, twenty-six—*

"Citizen!" slurped a man as he sidled up to Villane. "Citizen, the ramparts are fallen, the trumpets sounded and the armies bouncing through Cityside. Beware!"

Villane tried to step around the man. But he seized Villane's arm and, looking covertly from side to side as if afraid of being heard or seen, persisted. "Biobombs aren't enough! We need," he continued, his voice lowering and his eyes narrowing, "we need knives. Self-defense. Cityside. Defense the city. Knife the self!" The man threw back his head and roared. Villane tore his arm free of the man's grasp, shoved him aside and walked on, not looking back, alarmed and infinitely sorry for the man and what had created him. *Forty, forty-one—*

He had circled the arena and found himself back with Ruth and the others on his three hundred and eighty first step. He shook his head to answer the unspoken but evident question nestling in all their eyes.

Grandsir moaned and slumped down on the floor. "She's gone. Gone." The word lingered in the air like an idictment but of whom or of what, Villane could not tell.

He had no time to speculate further because the shouts of the psychs surrounding them suddenly grew louder and he turned to look out into the arena, searching for the cause of this new noise that threatened to shatter his ears and invalidate his senses. He found it. Ominously, the far wall of the arena was sliding slowly open to reveal a vast expanse of open and seemingly unguarded area beyond. The occupants of the turrets, Villaine saw, were suddenly active. An electric crackling filled the air for a moment and then was replaced by the sound of a Priestman's voice shouting instructions over the speaks. "Psychs, forward!"

The shouts grew louder. Fear became a viable presence in the arena.

Like a great mindless herd, the psychs stampeded, most of them, toward what many of them thought was freedom. A few hung back either through indifference or suspicion.

"I don't like it," York muttered.

Villane didn't either. He knew what was about to happen and he suspected that the others also knew. Everyone knew what had happened to psychs on their ill-fated passage from the civility of Cityside down through the dark corridors of pain and terror that emptied their contents at last into the Dump and then—beyond.

"Phillip," Ruth began, "is it—are we going to be sent out—out there?"

Villane wished that he could tell her no, that he could honestly deny what he knew lay ahead. He could not bring himself to answer but his failure to do so was an answer in itself.

Priestmen entered the arena, eyes glowing with a sense of mission. They prodded the reluctant psychs toward the ominous openness. Kicks. Clubs.

York was the first of the four to feel the wrath of the Priestmen as they pounced upon him and sent him reeling toward the place where the wall had once been. Villane struggled in vain as they seized him and hurled him after York. He turned to cry out to Ruth and, as he did so, he saw her being rudely flung toward him by one of the Priestmen. Two others lifted Grandsir and dragged him, unresisting, toward the open area.

"Forward, psych!" bellowed a Priestman materializing beside Villane, his club raised threateningly.

Villane moved out toward the others milling about in the open area under the always blue sky. Ruth joined him. She was supporting Grandsir, his arm thrown carelessly over her shoulder. She let Villane assume her human burden.

The Priestmen in the control turret vented the dome and deactivated the heat field. Sweat bubbled on Villane's brow and trickled down his spine as he moved forward with the mass of men and women embarking on the journey that not one of them wanted to take.

They passed out of the sunlight of Cityside, Villane and his three companions, and into the night of Limboland. They did not speak. They did not look back. As if in unspoken agreement, they kept their faces resolutely turned to whatever lay lurking in Limboland and farther on in Landsend. They did not look back, any of them, at what had once been and now would never be again because they knew that what they had left was lost to them and what lay ahead was life, however mysterious or murderous. They had no other choice.

When the last of the people had whimpered their way out of the Dump, the Priestmen inside pressed a collection of buttons and the dome descended like the teeth of a trap and the heat field sprang again into scorching life and consumed the several terrified psychs who ran back seeking safety, their hair flying and their arms flung out in front of them as if to receive gifts. They died like moths declaring their love of the light that only brought them instant and irreversible death.

Darkness.

As their eyes became accustomed to the black blanket enveloping them, Villane and the others looked back at the sprawling dome which glowed faintly like a gigantic firefly pregnant in the night. Severed now from the society in which they had been born, born again, this time into darkness, they felt the vastness of the otherness that was the world whose name was nightmare in the streets of Cityside.

They turned this way and that, unsure of what they were seeking, feeling their fingers grow cold and their voices dying in their throats as they became aware of the grim and bulky shapes moving like substantial shadows in the night and felt the angry eyes of those shadows watching them.

"Limbos!" cried Ruth in alarm.

"Sister!" Grandsir wailed, the word an incantation.

Growls or what sounded like growls, sounds without sense, were his only reply as the Limbos loped through the deep night and the psychs drifted away into the darkness and disappeared from sight as if they had never existed except in the minds of others who had merely imagined them.

"Take my hand," Villane said to Ruth. "York, stay close to us. Can you help me with Grandsir?"

"I can manage," Grandsir remarked unexpectedly. He removed his arm from Villane's shoulder.

"Stay close to us," York said to him. "We don't want to get separated."

"Join hands," Villane said. 'That way we'll be sure not to lose one another."

They formed a chain, each pulsing body a link in the chain, each weak, each weighed down by the knowledge of that weakness.

Villane spoke again in the darkness, sounding confident although he was not, sounding hopeful, although he could not let himself be. "We can't go back so we must go forward. Watch your step and follow me."

They moved out into the night that was new because it was real. They saw, for the first time, the stars so far above them and they were astounded by their beauty and their distance and they found them difficult to believe in, accustomed as they were to seeing all their lives those other electronic stars that blinked so relatively close in their circuited beds in the dome over Cityside.

Outcasts, they stumbled over stones and bumped into the skeletons of trees without leaves. Sweat was a lubricant on their joined hands and silence was, for a time, their only companion. Then the screams began, the cries that came like spears to pierce the shroud of the night surrounding them.

"What's that?" Ruth asked, terror tearing her voice.

"Don't know," Villane answered grimly.

York began fumbling about on the ground.

"York, what is it? What are you doing?" Villane squinted, trying to see York. He released Ruth and Grandsir and felt about in the dark for York. "Where are you? York!"

"Take it easy, Villane. Here."

Villane felt something thrust against his chest. He gripped it and felt rough wood. Part of it flaked away in his hands as he held it. "What is it?"

"Weapon," came York's curt reply. "Club. Better than bare hands."

The screams came and went, mixed with the growls they had heard earlier. The moon, like a flipped coin, slid out of the clouds and illumined the scene, making it not quite as bright as day.

York yelled, high and loud. He swung his club at the Limbo that leaped down upon him from the scarred trees and the naked creature fell to its knees, glaring up at him and seeking an opportunity to spring. Its cold eyes coveted York's throat where the blood pulsed warm and red. York swung again but the creature bounded away and was lost to sight.

Villane said, "We've got to get out of here and fast. We've got to get away from these things! Quick march! Forward, all of us!"

They sprinted under the moon and, after several minutes of a throat-searing pace, Villane slowed down and looked back over his shoulder. Cityside had vanished. They had come far. He felt no regret. Oddly, it seemed to him as if a burden had been lifted from his back. He found it easier to draw each breath although he was fully aware of the fact that each breath he now drew might be his last.

They found the first body a minute later. It had been a woman. Like an abandoned toy, it lay under the open sky, its limbs positioned as no human limbs, still alive, could possibly be, pieces of its flesh torn loose and carried away into the night that hid marauders and kept its secrets.

Ruth swallowed hard several times and turned away from the sight at her feet to hide her face against Villane's chest.

"Come on," Villane said. "Keep your clubs ready. Grandsir?"

"Here, boy. Lead on. I'll bring up the rear. My eyes are old and haven't seen it all yet, I guess. I'll watch."

Villane reasoned that the Limbos were incapable of making a distinction between the enemies of Cityside, the Landsenders, and the outcasts of Cityside. Perhaps there really was no difference. Perhaps we are as much enemies of Cityside as are the Landsenders, whoever and whatever and wherever they may be, he thought. Perhaps then it followed that there was a certain primitive logic in the behavior of the Limbos as they tore at their victims, classless and without visas in their territory, fair prey by reason of their ejection from Cityside. He almost laughed. He didn't. He walked on, occasionally whispering words of encouragement to the others, his thoughts vascillating between awe at the beauty of the night sky and fear of what else walked under that sky so near and so deadly.

"What time is it, Villane?" York asked.

Villane peered at the dial of his watch. He raised his wrist to his ear. The familiar *tock-tick* was gone. The crystal, he saw, was cracked. "Sorry, my watch is broken. It must have happened when the Priestmen grabbed me."

"The sky's getting lighter over there," Ruth observed. "It must be almost morning."

Grandsir said, "My old bones could use a bed. You think maybe it's safe to sleep somewhere around here?"

Villane pitied Grandsir but he firmly rejected the idea. He pleaded with him to keep walking. They had to get out of Limboland, he repeated. There had been other bodies, they had seen them lying bloody in the scragged bushes. Grandsir remembered didn't he? Grandsir said that he did and that he would continue walking but he wished they could go a little slower. Villane agreed to do so after warning him to keep his eyes as wide open as their lids would allow.

Dawn, when it came less than an hour later, was radiant. It looked down on the land and the four people it supported and did not seem to mind the incinerated earth and the stunted, lifeless trees that threw their dead limbs like accusing fingers up into the air, mute witness to the devastation wrought by Cityside during its Allegiance Alerts.

"Landsend," stated York, looking around him.

"It's hot," Ruth said, wiping her forehead with the back of her hand.

"Feels like summer," Grandsir observed. "But back home—back there—the calendar said it was February."

"But it's certainly summer out here," Villane said. "Why, it's only early morning and already it's getting hot. We must have been wrong in Cityside. It just can't be February."

York laughed and sat down, propping himself against a tree. "Remember our conversation about fact and fantasy, Villane? Cityside says it's February and so, by God, it's February! That's all there is to it. Never mind that out here summer's simmering in the land. God, how funny and how supremely absurd! Our sheltered little life back there was more of a circus than any of us ever knew if we choose to view circuses as having little or nothing to do with reality."

"And out here," Villane said thoughtfully, "everything's real. Is that what you mean?"

"Yes, that's just what I mean. Out here, nature defeats art. Summer comes when it's supposed to come and nobody's able to hold it back or at bay, calendars notwithstanding. That pleases me."

"This?" Ruth asked, gesturing at the bald landscape. "*This* pleases you, York? How could it?"

"You misunderstand me, Ruth. But it's unimportant."

Ruth stared at him for a long moment and then turned her attention to Villane. "We've got to find someplace to —well, hide, I guess. And we've got to get something to eat. I'm starved."

Villane looked helplessly around him. There was no serviset, no food to be seen or any practical way of finding any as far as he could determine. How helpless are the civilized, he thought, when the trappings of civilization—the servisets and the scanscreens, the aeroautos and electricity—disappear. Technology bore us in her scientific womb and never bothered to teach us how the parts of her body worked, certainly not why, and now, here we are delivered from that marvelous womb, renounced and rejected, ready to die of our disease called ignorance.

The sun rose pale and yellow and touched them with

its fingers of light and heat as they spread out, the four of them, to search for food and water. They found very little —a bush with green berries on it that looked singularly unappetizing and a tree from whose trunk there still trickled a thin sap. They put their mouths to the tree and tasted the sap. It had a cool, slightly sour taste, not altogether unpleasant and it was wet and their throats were parched. They sucked the sap with the same relish with which they had once drunk the finest wine their servisets could produce. They chewed the berries and were immediately and wretchedly sick. It was Grandsir who stumbled upon the small animal shivering in its burrow. It was small and brown and had two long ears. They did not know it was a rabbit. They did know it was meat. When Grandsir suggested killing it, they hesitated at first. But their hunger was a stern dictator and York's club did the job. They ate the rabbit raw. Ruth was sick again.

"I'll get used to it, I guess," she said later, when she had recovered. "It's just that it tasted so *alive*."

As the morning died and afternoon was born, they trudged on through the devastated land without meeting another living person. They saw sandy wastes and, once, a blue flower that had already begun to wilt under the sun's strong breath. They were totally unprepared for what they discovered on the other side of the hill as they descended, breathing heavily from their unaccustomed exertion.

It was not quite a village anymore. Its buildings were crumbling. Roofs had fallen in. Streets were indistinguishable amidst the rubble everywhere. Gaping hole like huge mouths yawned in the walls of the houses and over everything lay a thick layer of ashes, a micro-miniaturized version of the fragments of bricks and broken glass that littered the area.

"Shelter," Grandsir sighed.

"Careful," Villane warned, "it might be a trap."

"There's no one there," Ruth argued. "Let's go down and see what it's like."

Villane let himself be talked out of his reluctance and

he continued down the slope with the others. Uncertainly, like pilgrims unsure of what their welcome might be, they climbed over the heaps of rubble and stood at last in front of a frame house whose paint had blistered and flaked away, exposing its bare, scorched boards. Its roof was nearly intact but its windows were missing except for a few remaining shards of glass sticking out like dirty knives.

Villane went up to one of the windows and peered inside. He beckoned to the others to join him. "That must be furniture!" he murmured, pointing.

They gazed in at the broken sofa that lay in the room like a wounded elephant, its intestines—its springs—exposed. Wooden chairs lay splintered on the floor. An old coal stove caused speculation as to its possible purpose.

"Look!" cried Ruth, pointing to the torn calendar that still hung on one wall. "The date!"

"2001!" exclaimed Grandsir. "Why, I was darn near a boy that year! Look," he yelled joyfully, "December! See that date, the 25th, that red day there! That was Christmas back then."

"Christmas?" Villane asked. "December 25th is Salvation Day." Was Grandsir growing confused again, he wondered.

"Salvation Day indeed!" Grandsir spat. "Boy, you listen to me for a minute. Back then and for centuries before that even, December 25th was *Christmas,* you hear me? Like everything else, the Priestmen changed it, called it Salvation Day in honor of the birth of Cityside which they claimed took place on that day."

"I know, Grandsir," Villane said, 'but—"

Grandsir interrupted him and explained about Christmas, about presents, about evergreens, and when he had finished he swore vehemently. He sat down on the broken porch beside the still hanging but lopsided swing as the others went inside to explore the house. So many years, he thought, rummaging about in the trunk of his memory that the calendar, a rusty key, had unlocked. Christmas. He had been given a genuine meerschaum pipe one year shortly before Earth War Three. He remembered the smell of tobacco smoke and the feel of his teeth tight on the stem of that lost pipe. It had been a beautiful pipe and it had pleasured him greatly in those other days when the veins had not been visible beneath the skin of his hands. When his head had been full of dreams and his heart full of love for a woman long ago gone and almost forgotten now as if she had never actually been alive in their warm bed with him on the long nights when the snow fell outside and a sleepless owl hooted, its eyes seeking field mice.

He got up and walked down the desert that had once been a lawn, thinking of iced tea and recalling picnics and seeing, instead of the sun, sparklers and skyrockets on a once-upon-a-time Fourth of July.

He did not hear the soft singing at first as he swam in his sea of remembrance. But gradually it penetrated his consciousness. A small voice, out of tune. And something else. Something he had not quite forgotten. God, he thought, a piano! Where? He spun around like a hound who hears the hunter's horns and goes flying in search of the fox. Over there! In that shambles of a dwelling place that might once have been filled to overflowing with love and laughter. He began to run. The faster he ran, the harder beat his heart. He reached the open doorway and gazed, blinking, into the gloom. *"Sister!"* he sighed.

She sat there on the windup stool, her legs inches above the tilting floor and pecked with her two index fingers at the yellowing ivory keys of the upright piano looming in front of her. She did not hear his breathless saying of her name.

"Sister!" he cried.

She leaped from the stool, sending it crashing to the floor and her eyes widened with fear. She pulled a kitchen knife from her belt and then she saw who it was who had spoken. Incredulity battled with longing in her tense face. The knife in her hand fell to the floor. Her hands clenched. "Grandsir?"

"Oh, yes!" he cried. "Yes, yes. It's me. I'm *here!*"

Sister flew across the room to him and for a long delicious moment they were one person, their four arms defining the total expanse of their universe—their own two trembling bodies. Grandsir's fumbling fingers touched the rough scab that closed the wound above her ear. Then they laughed and they talked at once, stopped, asked questions, looked into each other's eyes, and laughed again.

Sister: "How did you—?"

Grandsir: "How did you—?"

"I teleported."

"I ran."

"Oh, I'm so glad you're here," Sister cried, hugging Grandsir as if he were a treasured toy. "It's terrible here. Have you seen them yet?"

"Who?"

"The Landsenders. Have you?"

"No. Where are they?"

Sister pointed to the floor. "Down there is where they are. Under the ground. Except at night when they all come out."

"The Landsenders?"

Sister nodded. "They're terrible."

"Come on," Grandsir said, seeing anxiety twist her features. "Let's go and join Ruth and York and Villane. Now we're all together again!"

"Yes," Sister said soberly. "That's good. Oh, Grandsir, I'm so glad you found me! I've been so scared!"

Grandsir took her hand and they headed back toward the house which held Villane and the others. Sister skipped. She laughed and called out to the empty air that she was coming, that she was alive and, oh, how good everything was going to be from now on.

Villane came out on the porch and saw them approaching. At first, he could not believe in Sister's evident existence, certainly not in her actual presence here and now. "Hey!" he yelled, a greeting to Sister and a summons to Ruth and York. "Hey, look who's here!"

Ruth ran out, paused a moment, and then ran down

the steps and seized Sister in her arms, lifting her high off the ground, both of them laughing as if at some secret joke they shared.

York, standing next to Villane, said, "Glad to see the kid's okay. I'd about given her up."

"Me too," Villane said. "I figured the Limbos had gotten her. Or worse." He bent down and kissed Sister's forehead as she came up to him. "You from the Dump?" he asked, in mock seriousness, repeating her question that she had put to him that long ago day when he arrived in Pume's apartment.

"Yes," she replied, her eyes twinkling. "Isn't everybody?"

"All of us, anyway," Villane admitted. "Come on inside."

When they were all together in the cluttered living room, Villane asked Sister, "What do you know about this place? Have you seen anyone? Heard anything?"

"Plenty," Sister replied. "There's people, sort of, out here. Only they don't look exactly like people and they act pretty funny. They live down under the ground and they only come out at night sometimes. I used to hide. They scared me."

"We'd better arm ourselves," York said. "No telling what weapons the Landsenders have. They may be rather difficult adversaries."

"Arm ourselves?" Grandsir asked. "With what?"

"Clubs for one thing," York replied. "We'll have to improvise something." He glanced around the room, trying in his imagination to transform the broken chairs and falling down doors into defensive weapons.

They spent the rest of the afternoon fashioning their arsenal. The results were primitive. They had searched the house and found a hammer and hatchet. Using these, they had loosened the metal handles on the coal stove doors and stamped and pounded them into pointed prongs which they then rubbed against the broken flagstones in the yard until their points were sharp. Then, using twine they had found in a filthy kitchen cupboard, they tied the prongs to the ends of chair rungs. Spears.

They made their way down the rotting steps into the dank basement of the house. There they found corroded buckets which had once held coal. They filled these with shards of broken glass from empty bottles that they had found on the basement floor and had taken from the windows on the floors above.

York, using every bit of his strength, bent a coal shovel around a large stone, creating a potentially effective club.

In their foraging, they found several containers with charred traces of paper clinging to them. It was Grandsir who recognized them as a source of food. He told the others about the way food had been packaged in cans in the days before the servisets and Cityside. He peered at the remaining fragments of the labels on the cans they had found but he was unable to determine from them the contents of the cans. He searched the kitchen until he found an ancient can opener. The cans yielded creamed corn and pears and apple sauce. They ate, marveling at the strange tastes, sickened slightly by the unfamiliar odors and the pungent juices that were like nothing they had ever known on their tongues or in their stomachs during their days in Cityside.

Later, the sun disappeared as clouds crowded the sky. Ruth and Sister went outside to stare up at this new thing, a sky without a sun. It made them vaguely uneasy but Grandsir had assured them it was perfectly normal here. What was abnormal, he had insisted, was Cityside's sky with its constant sun.

Villane, inside the house, heard Ruth's scream that came several minutes later. He raced to the door and bounded out onto the porch. He recoiled in surprise at the sight of the watery world that met his gaze. Ruth and Sister stood in the middle of the yard, paralyzed with fright, their hair streaming wetly down upon their foreheads.

Villane battled with himself, trying to muster courage to go to them. He took a tentative step and halted as

Grandsir came out of the house behind him and began to laugh.

Villane wanted to hit the old man. How could he laugh as Ruth and Sister suffered and he, a willing but all too weak warrior, tried to find the nerve necessary to go to their aid.

"Oh, oh," moaned Grandsir, holding his arms tightly against his body, almost doubled over with racking laughter. "Ruth," he called at last. "Sister. It's just *raining*, that's all!"

"What?" Villane gasped. "What's *raining*?"

Grandsir did not answer at first but went out into the downpour and gathered Sister up in his arms and took Ruth's hand and led them both back up on the porch. He deposited Sister on the porch and patted Ruth's shoulder. "Come inside. I'll explain."

After they had dried themselves with scraps of cloth, Grandsir told them about rain, something that had never occurred in Cityside. He did not care that they doubted the truth of his words as he told them how, when he had been a boy, he used to put on his bathing suit in summer when the rains washed the earth and how he had danced about like a dervish and shouted with joy as he sailed makeshift boats down gutters that had turned into minor rivers and how he had stood under apple trees and shaken their branches, happily drenching himself with rain and blossoms. Then, as they cowered before him when the lightning flashed and the thunder followed, he tried to convince them that what was happening was good and that the unfamiliar, the unknown and undreamed of, was not necessarily something that must automatically be feared.

The sun returned an hour later and Villane, like the others with the single exception of Grandsir, felt relieved at the return of the familiar and the withdrawal of the unknown that had brought with it brief moments of terror.

Night came and the group of people in the house huddled close to one another in the darkness only partly pierced by the light of the nearly full moon, waiting for what Sister had predicted—the appearance of the Landsenders.

They came. Their arrival was heralded by a kind of keening that burst out into the night like a noisy, unknown bird.

Sister was the first to hear it. "Here they come!" she cried, grabbing Grandsir's hand.

Villane got up and went to the broken window through which drifted the sound and the softness of the night air. He stood to one side, looking out. The keening rose and fell away and rose again. It reminded him of something. Something so familiar that he had difficulty at first identifying it. But then recognition came to him. The keening sounded very much like the whine and wail of the bombs that hurtled out from Cityside into Landsend with the regularity of Allegiance Alerts. The very familiarity of the sound brought him a strange sense of relief as he gazed out on the moonscape beyond the walls of the house in which they hid.

The sound suddenly increased in intensity. Villane realized why as he saw the mounds of earth lifting like thick lips opening. Out of the openings crawled the dim shapes of the Landsenders. Villane stared and beckoned to the others to join him at the window. As far as their eyes could see, the earth was opening and vomiting forth people, vaguely distinguishable in the light of the moon.

As they watched, the Landsenders, still keening, shambled off into the night that seemed to shelter them. Their bodies were clothed in garments of ragged cloth and fur. Hair grew thick on their heads and on the faces of the men. Some of them were missing limbs and hobbled on makeshift crutches. Others displayed scarred and burned bodies and faces. Many had bound their feet in rags but just as many others walked barefooted through the dirt. They looked neither to the right nor the left as they walked, each with his hands on the shoulders of the figure in front of him in the long line winding up the hillside.

"Where are they going?" York asked.

Sister said, "They go the same way every time. They

go up on that hill there and then you can't see them anymore."

"Look there!" Villane said. "What's that?"

They stared at the small figure being led by the last man in line, a rope around its neck, its hands bound and a dark hood tied over its head.

"I'm going to follow them," Villane announced.

They argued with him. Ruth pleaded with him to stay and when he refused, when he tried to explain that he needed to know what was going on in order to prepare himself and them for what might yet come, she grew angry and called him a fool determined to endanger them all. Villane accepted the insult which he recognized as the illegitimate offspring of Ruth's concern for his safety.

York volunteered to accompany Villane. They ordered the others to remain in the house until they returned. Ruth threw her arms around Villane and tried one last time to persuade him to change his mind. Gently, he freed himself from her embrace. Followed by York, he stepped out onto the porch and into the night, both of them carrying their homemade spears.

"We'd better hurry if we're going to catch up with them," York said. "I can hardly hear them anymore."

They raced off in pursuit of the fading sound. After several minutes, they glimpsed the procession winding its way like a determined snake up the side of the hill that shielded one side of the village. Keeping a safe distance between themselves and the Landsenders, Villane and York tracked the procession, coming at last to a clear plateau that seemed to have been hacked out of the hill's summit. They knelt down behind a pile of rocks and watched as the figures before them formed a large ellipse and two groups of people formed curious patterns that decorated each end of the ellipse. Villane, from his vantage point, whispered excitedly to York, "They've formed the outline of a biobomb! See, there are the wings of the bomb, those people up at the far end. The cluster nearest us represents the fuse load."

York whistled softly in the darkness. "You're right!"

They watched in silence as the small hooded figure was led into the center of the ellipse. A near naked woman stepped forward and the others moved closer together to close the gap in the ellipse that had been left by her departure. She untied the hood from the head of the figure before her. Villane and York realized with a profound sense of shock that it was a young boy who seemed to be no older than seven or eight. The woman turned from the boy and raised her arms and then dropped them. At once, small hand-held fires flared at various points of the ellipse, most of them clustered in the bottom of the bomb outline.

The keening grew into a scream—ululating, frenzied. The boy trembled as the woman turned to him and raised her hand above his head. In her hand, something gleamed.

"Sorrreeee, sorrreeee!" she wailed.

"What's she saying?" York whispered.

Villane shook his head, watching the woman and the grotesque scene being enacted before his astonished eyes.

" 'cept Hagel!" came the woman's cry. "Accept him, first fruit of Len and his woman."

Down came the gleam that was the knife. Up went the boy's stricken scream. Around whirled the resumed keening as the boy's blood splattered the flesh of the nearest spectators. As his body fell, the woman flung the bloody knife from her and screamed, "Sorrreeee! Sorrreeee! Forgive us our aggressions!"

Like marionettes the people moved forward and set up poles that had been lying on the ground. They quickly draped a sheer cloth over the poles and fastened it to the ground by placing stones along its ragged edge after the woman had bent down and placed a pot of glowing fire beside the boy's body lying so still beneath the cloth.

Then, in silence, the people flowed down the hillside.

When they had all gone, Villane stood up. He said to York, "They killed that child. I wonder why."

"Sacrifice," York stated flatly. "Don't you see, Villane? Don't you recognize that thing down there?"

Villane stared and thought and the thoughts that came to him were frightful. He began to understand what York had already guessed.

Speaking slowly like a man who has just discovered the ability to pronounce words, he said, "That's an imitation of Cityside down there—the dome! They've sacrificed to *Cityside!*" He fumbled for words to clothe his half-formed thoughts. "To protect," he continued, "to protect themselves probably from the bombs. They're trying to placate Cityside. They're *savages!*"

"We'd better head back," York said.

They picked their way down the side of the hill, saying nothing, alone with the thoughts that crawled about in their brains like loathsome night things possessing no utterable name.

When they arrived back at the house, they first scanned the immediate area for any trace of the Landsenders. Finding none, they made their way toward the house and went inside. They had to call several times before Ruth finally emerged from the basement, followed by Sister and Grandsir.

"What happened?" Ruth asked, rushing to Villane. "What did you see?"

Villane told them, sparing none of the gory details despite the revulsion he saw on Ruth's face as he described the ritual he had just witnessed. "So my guess is," he concluded, "the Landsenders have regressed to some primeval state in which they live in fear of Cityside and the devastation they know comes from there. They were saying—singing, sort of—that they were *sorry.*"

"Sorry for what?" Sister asked. "What did they do?"

"I'm not sure. But I'd guess that they are saying they're sorry for Earth War Three. Perhaps they or their ancestors started it or helped to start it. Some of them anyway. They probably think that they are being punished with biobombs and all the rest for that misdeed. They're apologizing for their offense by making sacrifices to the powers—the god or gods—that hold their very lives in their hands."

York paced the length of the room, shaking his head. "They were asking forgiveness for their *aggressions*."

Grandsir giggled. The others gazed at him, startled. "It's funny when you come down to think on it," he said pensively. "What I mean is, Cityside's bustling about like a hen whose eggs have been hidden, building bombs, bigger and better ones, all the time. And out here the enemy —" He had to stop as he began laughing almost uncontrollably again. "The *enemy*," he continued, when he had caught his breath, "is scared stiffer than stone and instead of fighting back, makes sacrifices to the great god Cityside!"

"You know," Ruth began, "we never went out and looked at what we were fighting. We stayed safely inside the dome with our circuses and our bombs and our cozy status quo that was strangling us although most of us wouldn't admit it or didn't know it. I see what you mean, Grandsir, about being funny in a sad way."

"Like when the rain came," Grandsir said.

"What?"

"It's a lot like before when you and Sister were caught in the rain, Ruth. You'd never seen or felt rain before, never even heard about it. So you were scared. Just because the rain was beyond your experience, you automatically reacted as if it were something bad."

"Only it wasn't," Ruth observed.

"Only it wasn't," Grandsir repeated. "And Cityside's the same way. Afraid of something that's basically harmless. As harmless as a trapped toad."

"But," said York, still pacing, "the trouble is they don't know that and they haven't bothered to find out about what's out here beyond their dome."

"It's getting light," Villane commented. "We'd better get some sleep."

They climbed the stairs to the second floor of the house and lay down on the dusty beds as dawn banished the night and no birds sang anywhere.

Villane lay on his bed in one of the rooms and gazed up at the ceiling, thinking. Thinking that this world he had stumbled into twenty-seven years ago was a world of prisons. Cityside was a prison. The earth itself was a prison for the Landsenders. His own body was a prison as was his mind with its three cells labeled Past, Present and Future. And the prisoners! How strangely content they were, most of them. The prisoners safe in Cityside would not, he speculated, willingly exchange their comfortable cells for freedom if freedom meant a going out to find the rest of the world and a going in to the crevices of their own minds. No, Villane told himself, we treasure our prisons and call them by mystical names—progress and pleasure and sometimes love.

He drifted into a weak sleep, turning and tossing in his dreams as he did battle with an enemy that had no face and whose arms were bio-bombs and whose maniacal screams he recognized as his own.

Outside, the sun slowly rose and paid no attention as the first bomb flew grayly through the sky and dipped down to deliver its obscene kiss to the prone and helpless earth.

It erupted with an evil roar and flames spewed forth from it to eat with red tongues and white, livid lips of light at the few remaining stalks of trees and faded blades of grass.

Villane leaped from his bed. The terrors of his dreams were replaced by the terrors of this day that was suddenly alive with fire and falling plaster and crumbling walls. He yelled, "Ruth!"

He ran out into the hall to find them all already there. Sister was crying, her head hidden in Grandsir's trembling hands. Ruth held a hand on each swaying wall that defined the narrow hall. York raced downstairs and Villane guided the others down after him.

"They must be having an Allegiance Alert!" York yelled back.

Villane realized that York was running but without a destination. He guessed that York was as frightened as the rest of them and, like a man knowing that he must act but not how, he was caught in a web of momentary madness. "York!" Villane shouted.

York stopped in his tracks and turned, the corners of his mouth moving, his eyes wide and fearful.

Villane went up to him and spoke softly but firmly. "Get hold of yourself. Steady up!"

Another roar outside. The house shuddered and tilted crazily. First came the sifting snow of plaster and then a beam broke free and fell with a crash, narrowly missing Villane where he stood, his hand on York's arm. He swung around and ran back to where Ruth crouched with Grandsir and Sister beneath the ceiling that was about to fall on them all.

"Outside!" Villane yelled. He guided them through the suffering house and made the choice that was not really a choice at all. "We're going underground," he announced.

He was relieved to hear no protests. He knew that, when one must choose between horrors as they were now doing, one does not make careful or calculated distinctions between the varying degrees of those horrors. He knew that, when life must be saved, the possibility of death must be sternly denied. "Search for one of the openings in the ground!" he commanded as they ran with him from the house. "We've got to go down or die!"

Sister stopped crying. She stopped moving. She vanished.

"Sister!" came Grandsir's anguished cry.

The house seemed to sigh and, like an aging and wrinkled woman who knows she will never have another lover, let go its hold on life and collapsed with a crash.

Trees became torches. The air was filled with the voices of the bombs as they fell and fell.

Sister's voice suddenly rose above the monstrous sound. "Here! Over here!"

Villane whirled around to spot her head and shoulders sprouting out of the ground like some strange flower. Her right arm was raised above her head, propping open one of the entrances to the underground world of the Landsenders.

They ran to her and, one by one, stumbled down the crude steps they discovered cut out of the hard dirt beneath the trapdoor. Villane was the last to go down and, as he lowered the trapdoor above his head, he said a mental goodby to the madness above and steeled himself to meet whatever new madness might be awaiting them here below the tortured skin of the earth.

Sister's voice came to him out of the dank blackness. "I teleported down here. I was afraid we'd never find the way in time."

"You were magnificent!" declared Grandsir. "Where are you, child? Can you find my hand?"

"Thanks, Sister," Villane said. "You did well."

"Phillip." Ruth's small voice came out of the darkness and Villane welcomed it as he would have welcomed a bright beacon held in a friendly hand.

"Over here, Ruth."

They found each other and continued moving down and down, the roar of war fading as they descended. The steps were steep. Their progress was slow. Fear walked with them and Villane felt suspended between two worlds, neither of which he wanted to live in but both of which were real and shouting to him to choose. He wondered if he would ever again walk on the earth or see the sun. He trudged along, fearing to fall, down the steps that led away from the sun, away from Cityside and away from all that was familiar but not necessarily safe or sane. His feet, as they moved clumsily down the steps, were learning a new language and his mind was discovering another of the infinite circuses that men devised to retain their sanity and shield their little lives from the danger of death that was never far away from the heart within the breast that some day would miss one too many beats.

"Villane?" It was York speaking.

"Yes?"

"I think it's getting lighter. Can you see anything?"

"Oh!" Ruth cried.

"What is it?" Villane asked anxiously as he felt her hand tighten on his own.

Before she had a chance to answer, he realized what had caused her to cry out. They had reached some kind of level or plateau. The steps ended abruptly and there were faint traces of light visible in the distance. The narrow walls that they had brushed with their shoulders during their long descent seemed to have vanished.

"Up there's where the light's coming from," Grandsir declared.

Now they could distinguish the outlines of their bodies in the flickering light that came from the end of the tunnel hollowed out of the earth.

They moved gingerly forward and came out of the tunnel into a large open area with other tunnels branching out from it in all directions. In the center of the area, in a deep pit, blazed a great fire which blinded them at first until their eyes became accustomed to its light. Its heat cancelled the dampness of the tunnel. The water dripping from the stalactites overhead fell into it with sputtering hisses.

At first, they heard what sounded like a muted shuffling. They discovered that it was not the sound of their own movements as they had at first thought when they saw the shaggy shapes of the Landsenders creeping toward them from the many mouths of the tunnels surrounding them.

Ruth drew back, bumping into York. Her shocked cry flew up and then fell like a wounded bird, "Phillip!"

In Cityside, the Priestmen stood penitent and suffered the violence of Pume's tirade in stricken silence.

"*Now* you tell me that you had them right in your grasp and you let them go!" Pume bellowed, stalking back and forth in the Interrogation Vault. "You fools!"

"Sir," ventured one of the Priestmen. "We did not let them go exactly. We *relocated* them along with the other psychs who were in the Depot at the time."

"Silence!" Pume screamed, his voice a shrill whistling. "No excuses. No explanations. Do not trouble me with facts. You claim that you did not receive my order. You dare to tell me that you did not differentiate between Villane and his band and the other psychs. You prattle of a misunderstanding. I despise you for the idiots you plainly are!"

The Priestmen clasped their hands reverently in front of them and bowed their heads.

Pume went on, more calmly, "So be it, then. They are gone thanks to your stupidity and my failure to know you for the incompetents you have clearly proven to be." He slapped his hands against his thighs in impotent rage. "They shattered my sound sender, you know, and even if I had another one it would be of no use now. They are undoubtedly dead or too far away by now for the signals to reach them."

"Perhaps we could—" a young Priestman began.

"Perhaps we could what?" snapped Pume. "Send a search party out into Limboland for them? Oh, ten times foolish! Well, I will have my revenge. If by some unlucky chance they still survive out there, it will not be for long. Priestmen, prepare an Allegiance Alert! Make it the biggest, the best and the longest yet! We will, at one and the same time, scourge them and destroy Landsend once and for all! Away!"

The Priestmen hurried from the room like rodents, leaving Pume to his fury and his frustration that sought a victim and found only empty air which he squeezed between his clenched fists as if it were guilty of some unspeakable crime. He left the Interrogation Vault and went back to his apartment where he threw open the windows and waited for the signal that would announce the beginning of the Allegiance Alert. When it came, he drew deep breaths into his lungs and smiled broadly as he listened with delight to the song the bombs sang as they tore out of the vented dome in search of his enemies.

Villane was seated on a thronelike dais carved out of solid rock. Beside him was Ruth. On his left, York, Sister and Grandsir all similarly enthroned.

"Villane," York whispered, "what's going on? You have any idea?"

Villane didn't. He shifted his position slightly and started to rise. Immediately, a thick-shouldered man stepped forward and grunted something that sounded like a command. His face and body were covered with dirt and so was his beard and his long hair.

"I think he means for us to stay put," York said.

Villane slid his hand across the arm of his throne and Ruth took it.

Suddenly, the music began. It was not really music. It was merely sound. Sound created by the people shuffling into the cavern, beating on makeshift drums and striking metal against metal to produce booming and tinkling sounds that provided a morose accompaniment to their ragged procession. They circled the fire three times and then dispersed to take up stations at various points in the cavern. There were at least two hundred of them.

The woman Villane and York had seen on the hillside during the sacrifice left the crowd and approached them. She seemed to move hesitantly, even fearfully. Her eyes were fastened on Villane's face. In her hands, she held a shallow dish made of stone. She continued to advance and after every four steps, she stooped slightly and stepped first to the left and then to the right in a bizarre little ballet.

"She doesn't look like she could hurt us," Villane whispered to York. "But I wish I knew what was going on."

The woman came within three feet of Villane. She traversed the remaining distance that separated them and knelt suddenly, lowering her head, her filthy hair falling down over her face, her body a nondescript lump. She placed the stone tray at Villane's feet.

Villane looked down at the wriggling white mass on the tray. The woman surreptitiously raised her head and then she reached into the writhing mass in the tray, extracted one of the white grubs and shoved it into her mouth. As she chewed, she gestured to Villane and then to the tray. She made harsh guttural sounds in her throat that sounded like the words that might be spoken by someone who has garbled the alphabet.

"Phillip," Ruth whispered. "She wants you to eat!"

Disgust twisted Villane's features. "I can't," he insisted.

"You'd better, Villane," York told him. "No telling what she'll do if you don't."

The woman lifted the tray and thrust it toward Villane. He reached out and took a grab, holding it wet and slimy between his thumb and index finger. He placed it in his mouth and swallowed it. Making a supreme effort, he managed to keep it down. He took another. The woman bared broken teeth in what might have been a smile. She rose and carried the tray from one to another of the group, not moving on to the next one until each of them had eaten from her offering.

Then she set the tray down and turned to the people assembled in the cavern. Raising her arms, she began to speak. "Ar offering 'cepted by god things. Rahjoice, mens! Rahjoice, womens!" Turning back to Villane, she bowed and said, " 'cept our gratefuls for you come. Usall beg you peace!"

Villane did not know what to do or say. Clearly, something was expected of him. The woman—all people in the cavern—seemed to be waiting like patient animals for him to make some sign, some movement, say some magic word that they yearned for in evident desperation. He stood up on somewhat shaky legs and the woman drew back. The people watched him with glinting eyes. "Thank you," he murmured weakly, and sat down again.

Drums were beaten and the clumsy cymbals sounded.

"Rahjoice, mens!" the woman cried, waving her arms. "Rahjoice, womens! Rahjoice, usall!"

The woman beckoned and a man stepped forward. He gestured toward Villane and the others and began to lope toward one of the tunnels leading from the cavern. He stopped, turned, gestured again.

"I guess we'd better follow him," Villane said.

"We haven't much choice," Grandsir commented.

They trooped after the man, the people folding back

upon themselves to make way for their passage, their heads lowered, only a few of them daring enough to steal a glance at them as they entered the tunnel lighted by flaring torches fastened to the walls.

They walked for several minutes until they came to another tunnel that intersected the one they were in at right angles. Their guide turned and muttered something.

"Did he say 'temple'?" Ruth asked in a low voice.

"I'm not sure," Villane answered.

Their guide stopped and pointed to an erect stone slab covered with ochre dye of some sort. "You goes," he muttered, shielding his eyes from the sight of the stone. "Usall stay. *Temple.*"

"Thanks, thank you," Villane said.

The man ran rapidly back the way he had come and disappeared.

York stepped up to the stone slab and ran a forefinger along its rough surface. The ochre dye stained his finger. He leaned closer and examined the slab. "Look here, Villane."

Villane joined him.

"The ellipse again. A crudely drawn bomb."

"A symbol of sorts," Villane said. "A symbol of their lives and the thing that determines and can terminate their lives. Well, let's see what's behind it."

They stepped around the slab and walked a few paces. They soon found themselves in another large area, dimly lighted by torches and heavy with the scent of burning pitch.

"C'mon in, fellow god things!" a voice welcomed them. "How's it feel to be resurrected and worshiped?"

"Who are you?" Villane asked the man approaching them from the far end of the giant room.

"Me? I'm Danzech. You?"

They introduced themselves. Villane asked, "What are you doing here? How'd you get here?"

The man laughed a little and held up his hands and pursed his lips. "Hey, one at a time. One question at a time." He pointed to the floor. "Let's make ourselves comfortable first. C'mon over here."

He led them to the center of the room which was littered with wooden crates and rotting paper cartons that bore the anachronistic legends SUNKIST and SMIRNOFF'S and other names. "Now," he said, when they were all seated on cartons or rocks, "I told you who I am. I'm from the Disposal Depot. You too, I bet."

"That's right," Villane admitted.

"Not many of us get through," Danzech said solemnly. "Takes a little luck. Guts. Survival of the fittest."

Villane tried to overcome the feeling of distaste that gripped him as he listened to Danzech. But it was impossible. There was something repellent about the man. It was not just because he was dirty and unkempt. They all were now, more or less. Villane's own face was bushy with beard and Ruth's hair was a tangled net that seemed to have caught her head in its ragged clutches.

Danzech said, "The joke you just went through out there is the same as they give to every new god thing Cityside sends them although not many have been getting through lately. Or, if they have, they don't find their way down here. Anyway, like I been saying, those of us who do get through and down here get treated swell. See, the way I figure it is this. I figure these Enders—" He saw the puzzled looks they gave him.

"Enders is short for Landsenders, get it?" He guffawed, scratched himself found a flea and cracked it with a *snick* between his long fingernails. "They think, far as I can tell, that Cityside is a kind of god itself and so it stands to reason, don't it, that anybody who comes out of there must be a god thing too. Make sense?"

"Yes," Villane said. "I think I understand. Seems to me that these people are scared of their own shadows."

"Wouldn't you be? I mean with biobombs and Limbos all over and stuff. Wouldn't you be?"

"How long have you been here, boy?" Grandsir asked Danzech.

Danzech's eyes flared and his teeth clenched. "Boy?

Where do you get off calling me 'boy'? Didn't you hear me explain who I am? I'm a god thing! So shut your mouth on that 'boy' business!"

"He didn't mean any harm," Villane said quickly. "How long have you been here?"

"I been here a long time. Ain't no calendars or factclocks down here. A long time, I been here. Hear tell there's others too."

"Others!" Grandsir questioned, keeping his tone level and swallowing the word 'boy' that rose automatically to his lips.

"Yeah. These tunnels crisscross and spread out for miles as far as I can figure. The Enders talk about the *other* god things. Which is strongest. Which prettiest. You know."

Villane turned to York. "Maybe if we could find some of the others, we might be able to—"

"Never seen any of 'em," Danzech declared. "Who needs 'em anyhow? We got a good setup right here all for ourselves. Got enough to eat and drink and a place to sleep. No work to do. Who needs the others? Can't you smell a good thing when you come on it?"

Before Villane could comment, the attack began. The earth shuddered and dirt drifted down in a fine dry rain on them where they stood looking up and listening to the thunderous roar—the *thud-thud* and *boom*—of the bombs.

The Landsenders ran to and fro in the tunnels as Villane and the others took refuge beneath an overhang of solid rock that jutted out from one wall.

Danzech commented, "This is the worst yet! Cityside must have gone crazy! They must be trying to wipe us all out once and for all time to come!"

Villane, who had no frame of reference by which to measure the impact of the attack, held Ruth in his arms and kept silent, hoping that the ceiling would hold, fearful of being entombed alive here in the reverberating heart of the earth.

It lasted for what Villane judged to be hours during

which the terrified Landsenders gathered outside the "temple" and beat their drums and banged their cymbals and sang their entreaties. But the bombs fell and the "god things" were powerless to prevent the holocaust.

It ended finally, and Villane got up and went out to stand in front of the stone slab. He had expected to find the Landsenders there. They were gone. In front of the stone lay their offerings—brittle branches, a few withered leaves, berries. And the dead body of an infant. Villane raised his head, wanting to cry out in pain but he did not because he realized that there was no one to cry out to and nothing to cry. The senselessness of it all, the insanity of it all, overwhelmed him and he let himself sink into a morass of despair. Would Cityside never learn, he wondered. Would they never imagine alternatives to destruction? Villane felt himself become a part of the darkness while he yearned for light and reason and wondered if they were real or only the products of his own dazed mind that seemed to have no room left in it for anything but horror.

As he stood among the leaves and the berries, staring at the tiny lifeless body, he began to see that it was not enough to simply say no. Not enough to merely deny what was evil. No, there must be more, he told himself. The no-saying was but the first step. But after that first negative step must come positive ones, one after the other until the road was built and the journey taken. He looked around him, walked a little way toward the intersecting tunnel, looked down it, saw another tunnel and still another. He studied the ground under his feet and saw that there were steps leading down in two places. He had not noticed them before. Did the world of the Landsenders wind down and down, he asked himself, to the very hot heart of the earth?

Villane began to realize that it did not really matter where the tunnels led. What did matter, he thought, feeling a tinge of excitement and the first faint stirring of hope, was where the tunnels *could* lead. Feeling as if he had made a great discovery, taken a giant step forward, he ran back to confront his companions.

"Danzech," he began, "how do you call the Landsenders if you want them? Is there a way?"

Danzech nodded, pointing to a corner where a drum rested on its side. Villane went to it and picked it up. As he was about to leave, Ruth came up to him.

"What are you going to do, Phillip?"

"I have an idea. Wish me luck."

She placed her hands on his shoulders and kissed him lightly on the lips. "Luck."

Villane went out and began to beat on the drum with the palms of his hands. At first nothing happened and he was about to abandon his efforts but then the Landsenders began coming. In groups of two and three and alone, they crept into the tunnel. Villane could hear their heavy breathing as they waited, cowering, before him. He searched the faces before him as he thought of how he could turn the Landsenders and their energies to his own purpose. Eventually, he reasoned, it would be for their own good. He realized that the people standing so expectantly before him could not be changed overnight, perhaps not ever, certainly not now, this minute. For scores of years, they had been attacked by Cityside and they had begun to believe that there must be a good reason for the attacks made upon them. So they had postulated their own guilt, a theory based in part on fact. On the part of their participation—or their father's or grandfathers' participation—in Earth War Three. There was nothing for it, Villane decided, but to exploit this feat and sense of guilt if his plan was to work.

"Sister!" he called. To the people, he said, "Little goddess coming!"

Sister ran out of the temple and joined him. "You've got to help me," he whispered to her. "I'll explain later. For now, just do as I say." He told her what he wanted her to do but not why. He reminded her that the Landsenders were more afraid of her than she was of them.

They would not harm her, he assured her. She was, after all, a goddess. Sister agreed to the experiment.

"She," Villane said, pointing to Sister. "Powerful! Now!" he said to Sister who promptly disappeared. A cry went up from the rear of the crowd where Sister suddenly materialized. The people fell away from her, falling to their knees, shuddering. Sister vanished and reappeared beside Villane. For several minutes, she teleported here and there and then back again to stand beside Villane. It worked. Villane saw awe in the eyes staring at Sister. He drew her aside and told her what to say to the people. He told her to pretend that she was speaking to children, to keep her statements simple and to the point.

Sister stepped foward and Villane was pleased to see the confidence that manifested itself in the firm set of her shoulders and the calm expression on her face. Sister asked the Landsenders where the bombs came from. At first, they obviously thought she was asking where they fell. They pointed above their heads. Sister tried several more times, at last succeeding in making them understand that she wanted to know if they knew the location of Cityside. They pointed to the temple area. Sister looked questioningly at Villane.

"Good," he sighed. Addressing the crowd, he said, "I must return to my true temple. You must help me. I so command you!"

Feeling guilty about his method but determined nevertheless to use it because he knew of no other, Villane beckoned to the priestess standing in the front of the crowd. She came to him and he repeated his commands and told her what he wanted her people to do. When he had finished, she bowed before him and began to speak to the gathered crowd in a rapid, semicoherent language. During her short speech, Villane could understand a word or two here and there. He began to hope that his plan might work.

During the time that followed, a time without day or night or hours, the "god things" were billeted in a lower level cavern while the Landsenders began, fearfully at first, but goaded on by the priestess and Villane, to dig a new tunnel. Using crude tools fashioned out of rock and wood, they began to dig in the direction of Cityside.

At times, indecision seemed to seize the diggers. They would stop digging and begin arguing among themselves. At such times, Villane joined them, walking among them giving commands and insisting that he was anxious to return home to his heaven. The irony of his urgings did not escape him. He reminded the Landsenders of the powers manifested by Sister and they began to dig again.

He had just returned from the site of the digging when a far away cry shot down the tunnels and echoed in the earth. Other cries came and were followed by the sound of running feet and the sweaty smell of fear.

"What's happening?" York shouted to Villane. "It sounds as if they've gone wild!"

"Come on, let's go and find out," Villane said, already running.

They raced down the length of the tunnel and climbed the stairs leading to the upper level. There they saw the Landsenders running toward them in near panic. Villane drew himself up and held up his hands, a feeble barrier. They stopped and jabbered at him, throwing glances over their shoulders and pointing back in the direction from which they had just come runnnig.

At last, after persistent questioning, Villane was able to determine that part of the tunnel wall had collapsed. But this was not the major cause of the excitement; falling walls and crumbling roofs were part of the way of life under the earth. The Landsenders, he learned, had discovered new "god things!"

Villane raced down the tunnel with York. They made their way, crouching, through the new tunnel being hollowed out of the earth and came to the fallen rock and rubble. Standing bewildered in the midst of it, was a young girl wearing the tattered remnants of a white uniform that Villane immediately recognized as the kind he himself had worn during his employment in the Life Laboratory in Cityside. Beside the girl stood two men.

"I'm Phillip Villane," Villane said to the girl. "From Cityside."

"Hello," the girl said softly. "My name is Fan. This is Rourke and Jimmy. We've frightened your people, I'm afraid."

Villane introduced York and the five of them began to compare notes. Their experiences, they discovered as they talked, were parallel in nearly every respect. Fan and the two men had fought their way through Limboland and then had wandered through the desolation of Landsend before Fan had accidentally fallen through one of the open trapdoors set in the side of a hill. They had climbed down and discovered the Landsenders, learned to know what role they were unwittingly destined to play among these primitives and they had been living under the ground ever since. Like Villane and York, they had lost all conception of time. All any of them knew was the fact that it seemed like centuries since they had last seen the sun.

Villane told them about his plan in progress. Fan was enthusiastic about it but Rourke voiced reservations. Jimmy said that he thought it had definite possibilities. Eventually, they all agreed with Villane when he argued that it was at least worth a try and certainly better than living the rest of their lives like half-alive corpses buried in the earth and subsisting on sickening worms and bitter fruits. He reminded them that they had begun to grow thin and that their speech was often slurred and that their eyesight was weakening in the poor light. Was this what they wanted, where they wanted to remain? They at least would have a fighting chance if they worked their way back into Cityside.

"So what if we do get there?" Rourke protested. "The Priestmen'll shoot us down as soon as they see us."

"Maybe," Villane admitted.

"I'm not so sure I want to go back," Fan said.

Villane admonished her. "Don't make the mistake of

thinking that Cityside is now and always will be what we knew. Things change—"

"Sometimes for the worse," Jimmy interejcted.

Villane continued relentlessly. "Things change because people want them to change. I believe it's not enough to just reject Cityside and what it is. I believe it's up to people—you and me, for example—to change it. Take the good parts. Eliminate the bad parts."

His enthusiasm spread rapidly to the others. Fan was watching him with admiration and when he had finished speaking, she turned to Rourke and Jimmy. "Oh, I believe he's right! I really do. I can imagine what Cityside *could* be like."

"And I can imagine," Rourke put in, "what it would be like to get my hands on a few of those Priestmen."

"We could destroy the Dump!" York exclaimed, surprised at his own growing sense of excitement that sent the sweat trickling down his back although it was damp and cold in the tunnel.

"Let's go back," Villane suggested. "You'll want to meet the rest of us."

As time passed, other "god things" were discovered as new tunnels were unearthed. There were both men and women and nearly all of them came to share Villane's enthusiasm and endorse his plan. But there were those who, like Danzech, hung back and took no part in the digging because they were afraid and preferred to hold their little lives in their trembling hands here beneath the earth rather than risk them in the dreaded streets of Cityside again. But they were in the minority.

Soon there were more than a score of men Villane knew could be counted upon when and if they ever found themselves once again in the midst of the society that had so righteously rejected them. A kind of camaderie grew up among the men as they plotted and planned between digging sessions. Occasionally there was the sound of laughter, a sound nearly forgotten, like a rumor on the wind. Above all, there was hope, an eager fire fed by the energy of Villane's constantly voiced enthusiasm.

Villane went often to inspect the tunnel that ate its way toward Cityside like a voracious snake. He helped dislodge boulders and shore up the ceiling with stumps of trees brought down from the surface. His fingers often bled and more than one nail was missing from them.

The work went on. But questions nagged at Villane. How would he know when the tunnel was actually beneath Cityside? All he had to judge by was his own sense of the distance they had traversed between the Dump and the discovery of the destroyed village. What would they do without adequate weapons if they ever emerged once again in the streets of Cityside? Was his plan really as foolish as it sometimes seemed even to himself? Was it worthwhile? Would it—could it possibly—work?

It was during one of these times of doubt that Grandsir, guessing what was passing through Villane's mind, gave him the simple encouragement he so desperately needed.

"You're wondering will we make it," Grandsir stated, avoiding Villane's eyes. "Well, maybe we won't, boy, maybe we won't ever." Then, slyly, "I was talking to Danzech a while back and he's still complaining about our tunnel. Danzech thinks we ought to just stay put and let the world go by—or over, as is the case with us. Maybe he's right."

"He's not!" Villane almost shouted. "Danzech is a failure that walks like a man. He'll take today and let tomorrow go. He doesn't give a damn about what might make today more tolerable and thus tomorrow even better. I despise men like Danzech who let themselves be governed by what is and never by what might be!"

Grandsir expressed mock dismay. "Well, you got to admit he's got a point."

"He's got *no* point! No point at all. He reminds me of that animal you found up on top before we went down into the village. It just sat there shivering and let us catch it and kill it. It didn't fight back. It didn't try to change things. Not even by running away. That's Danzech for you!"

"It was weak and we were strong. It was scared."

"Sure, we're all scared. I'm scared sometimes so badly that I want to run down one of these tunnels and disappear forever and never have to face another person or think another thought as long as I live. And I'm weak. Cityside—Pume and the Priestmen—are strong. But, by God, Grandsir, I'm still a man and I'm going to stand up and act like one until I do what I have to do even if I die doing it!"

"Good for you, boy," Grandsir said quietly. "I'm with you all the way. If these old bones of mine can keep creaking on a while longer, I'll get to see just what you can make of yourself and the rest of us thrown into the bargain."

"I'm not a hero. But I just can't quit. I can't renounce the will and ability to act just because I'm scared and not very strong."

"None of us are heroes, boy. We're just stuffed with dreams and ideas. Got to act on 'em or they aren't worth having a'tall."

Villane started at the sound of his name being shouted aloud in the echoing tunnels.

"Villane! —*ane, ane, ane!*"

"That's York!" Villane said, heading for the tunnel. As he careened around a corner, he collided with York. They bounced apart and for a moment both of them were too stunned to speak. Then, recovering himself, York began to babble excitedly. Villane was unable at first to make any sense of what the man was trying to say. "Take it easy, York. Slow down! Now, what's this about pipes?"

"Villane, we've dug right into the water supply and sewerage system beneath Cityside! Come on, I'll show you. Hurry!"

Villane sprinted after York down the maze of tunnels toward the faint gurgling sound in the distance. Minutes later, he felt his feet sink into the soft, muddy earth. He had to slow down because of the sucking earth sluicing beneath his feet. But at last they reached the end of the new tunnel. Before them, looking like great gray veins, the pipes stood revealed in the damp flesh of the earth.

"Whew!" Villane breathed, staring. "You're right, York. We must be directly under Cityside. The water's coming from that leak over there. We'd better do something fast or we're all liable to drown down here."

"I've sent Ruth," York said, "to bring every Landsender she can find. We've got to start digging *up!*"

As the Landsenders came chattering excitedly into the tunnel, Villane explained what they must do. He described the angle of the graded slope they must make. At once, some of the Landsenders began to dig, others to carry away the dirt and deposit it in one of the tunnels farther back.

Ruth arrived. "Phillip—?"

Villane waved an arm. "That's the water supply system under Cityside," he told her. "We've made it!"

Ruth remained silent for a moment before commenting, "Now that we're this close, I'm not so sure I want to be. Fan has refused to come. I think I know how she feels."

Villane stared at Ruth and what he saw gave him pain. Her begrimed face and rough hands lent the lie to the beauty that he knew was hidden there somewhere beneath the film of dirt. The beauty that had stirred his body and bemused his mind almost from the first moment he had seen her standing so defiantly in Pume's laboratory. Only her eyes still seemed familiar. He said, "Think about what we're trying to do. Think about what the alternatives are. It's not really so important whether we win or lose. But we've got to try."

"I know."

Villane turned back to watch the Landsenders and the score or more of "god things" who had joined them tearing at the earth with their awkward tools and bare hands. He could stand his own inactivity no longer. Motioning to Ruth to remain where she was, he joined the frantic diggers, falling to his knees and clawing away at the earth, blinking when it temporarily blinded him. He kept on digging.

Grandsir and Sister arrived. No one bothered to replenish the pitch that fed the torches and the light gradually dimmed as the digging went on while blood flowed from fingers to feed the unfeeling earth.

There was no way of recording the passage of time just as there had not been throughout the entire unmeasured time of their existence beneath the ground. It might have been weeks. Months seemed much more probable. Only the demands of their bodies, the need for sleep and food, gave them any indication, and that an unreliable one, of the passage of time in this lower world where there was no day, no night, and no seasons.

Ruth fell asleep. A long time later, the cry of the men rocked her awake. "What—what is it?" she stammered, unable for an uneasy moment to tell where she was or even who she was.

They had broken through the roof of the tunnel and were scrambling down as they dodged bits of loosened rock that fell down upon them like a calcified rain.

Ruth threw up her hands to stop the pain in her eyes as light filtered down into the tunnel, clean and white and too bright to bear. Carefully, she peered through the web of her fingers. She rubbed her eyes as the others were doing and, like the others, heard the absolute silence in the tunnel as they all stared up at the hole that had been chipped through the cement barrier overhead. Occasionally, a stone fell *splat* into the rising water around them. Ruth moved forward and the wet earth covered her bare feet.

Villane said, "Rourke, you and Jimmy come up with the rest of us. Ruth, you stay here with Grandsir and Sister. Make sure that—"

"No!" Ruth scrambled past York and made her way on her hands and knees up to where Villane was staring out of the hole. "I'm going out too," she told him firmly. "I won't stay down here anymore."

Villane studied her, looking into her wide and wonderful eyes, and he said, "York, let her come." To Ruth he said, "Stay behind us. No telling what we'll run into or what we'll find up there." He took her hand and pulled her close to him. "I wish you were scared. Then maybe you'd stay down here where it's safer."

"I *am* scared. But I'd rather be scared *with* you than without you."

Villane was the first to haul himself out of the hole. York came next. They lifted Ruth out and then Rourke and Jimmy joined them, followed by most of the other men. The Landsenders cowered below, hiding their faces, beating their breasts and moaning.

They found themselves in one of Cityside's sector passages. Villane's forehead bled where he had been struck by a falling rock during their ascent. He paid no attention to the ruby drops that dripped down his cheek to fall on his naked shoulder.

He gazed around the empty passage. He stepped away from the mouth of the hole and began to walk slowly toward the end of the passage. The others followed him, their bare feet making no sound on the smooth pavement. Villane, when he reached the end of the passage, leaned forward and peered out. He could not believe what he saw. He had been prepared for guns or screams but not for the awful silence that seemed to have swallowed Cityside. There were no citizens to be seen, no Pricstmen. Carveyors stood motionless. Parked aeroautos sat driverless.

Villane calmly gave orders to the ragged band of men surrounding him. He dispatched small groups of men in several directions, silently wishing them well while worrying about the evident puniness of the clubs and makeshift spears they carried in their tense hands.

When they had gone, Villane moved out and on, Ruth and the others following him. They glanced into shop windows and saw no one. They looked up at apartment windows and saw no faces. They walked on, growing bolder. They passed the empty entrances to buildings and the vacant podiums where once Priestmen had stood. Villane made his way into one of the tiny public parks. York opened his mouth to call out to him and then promptly closed it. He watched Villane approach the factclock on the park wall and switch it on.

"Time 3:13. Nineteenth day, tenth month. Allegiance Alert continues. Work hard. Work wins."

Villane returned. "It's October!" he cried. "We've been below since February!"

"Correction," York said. "It wasn't February in Landsend. It was summer, remember? So out there now it must be July!"

"Almost a year!" Ruth exclaimed.

"I don't like this," Rourke declared suddenly, looking around him. "Where is everybody?"

They followed Villane as he made his way through the neat streets, heading they were not sure where. Suddenly, Villane stiffened. "Get back! Back against the wall!"

Up ahead stood a lone young woman. As they watched her warily, she barely moved. She leaned against one of the vacant podiums beside the motionless carveyor and they saw that her lips were moving as her thin hands feathered up and down her bare arms. Villane was within shouting distance of her and he was about to call to her when he thought better of it. He went up to her and was about to speak when he heard what she was muttering.

"Turn to the left. Walk down three blocks. Sensory Central. East side. Lost. Where is Central? Three blocks, left, turn to the east . . ."

Her voice withered away. Her eyes were as empty as the streets. She furrowed her brow and began to speak again, sounding as if she were reciting a lesson poorly learned. "Down three blocks but then which way?"

They left her. They walked on and came upon a man sitting in the middle of the street running one gnarled finger along the crack in the pavement as he rocked back and forth, humming softly to himself, totally unaware of their presence.

"Psychs," Ruth murmured.

Villane shook his head. "I don't think so. They'd be in the Dump. No, there must be some other explanation."

"There's the arsenal up ahead," York said, pointing. "We'd better steer clear of it."

But Villane marched toward it. Something seemed to draw him to its forbidding exterior. When he reached it, he put out his hand toward the ring in the door, paused momentarily and then seized the ring and pulled the unresisting door toward him. They entered the arsenal and walked through its empty halls and unpeopled rooms, hearing the hum and whirr of hidden machinery.

They hesitated briefly before the door labeled *War Room* and then entered to watch in silent shock the automatically operated bombardiers reach out their delicate mechanical claws, pick up a bomb, place it gently in its cradle, recoil, press the red button to send the bomb hurtling through the vented dome, return and pick up another bomb, place it in its cradle, recoil press the red button . . .

Click, clack, buzz. Clickety-hiss went the hoses spewing out the lethal gas. *Pick, place, press* went the uncaring claws of the bombardiers.

Villane almost staggered as he watched the ghastly ballet being danced and heard the oily song being sung by the efficient bombardiers. He wanted to laugh. Or cry. Or curse. The absurdity of what was happening filled him with disgust. The machines did what they had been programed to do and now that their trainers had gone away the machines went on doling out death with never a protest or a pause. Villane leaped forward as if he were about to attack the senseless metal maze. He searched until he found the computerized control center and he shattered it with a single blow of his bare fist. The ball ended and the song died as the bombardiers' claws stopped clicking and the bombs remained arrested in their cradles. He silenced the obscenely hissing hoses.

"Where the hell *is* everybody?" York yelled.

Villane thought he knew. "Sensory Central," he said calmly.

They made their way there. As they stood outside the shining building, Ruth pointed to the stains on the steps. "That looks like blood."

Villane bent down for a closer look. Rising, he said, "It is."

Inside, they found the citizens. Dozing and drifting in their electrolytic slumber, they shuddered and smiled and groaned and grimaced as the spools spun soundlessly in their sockets, spilling dreams. Whenever a spool ended, the occupant of the pallet rose up, selected another from the disordered pile by his pallet without bothering to look at it, plugged it in, lay back and closed his eyes.

Villane felt regret and a deep sadness wing down upon him as he gazed upon the mass tomb that was Sensory Central. Here, he reasoned, was the new Disposal Depot where sanity survived only through the false grace offered by unreality that spun on spools and along the wires to the electrolytic pins that sprouted from the flesh of the citizens like a steel gray and glistening moss.

Villane spun around and spoke to York. "You remember that they vented the dome when the psychs were driven out of the Dump?" York nodded and Villane went on, his decision made, his vote cast. "There must be a way to roll back the dome altogether. Think you can find it?"

"I'll find it," York assured him, turning to go. "It's probably controlled from the Dump."

Suddenly, a Priestman appeared in the doorway. "No more room!" he shouted angrily. "Come back next week!" Then, eyes widening, he cried, "Who are you? Where—?"

"Grab him!" Villane yelled. He lunged for the Priestman and they fell, struggling, to the floor.

As the Priestman's gun went off, the sound shot *pinged* through the still air of the room. Villane twisted the Priestman's arm and yelled for help. York sprang forward and struck the Priestman a stunning blow on the side of the head. Villane stood up, retrieving the Priestman's gun from where it had fallen. He was about to say something when the slip-slapping of boots in the hall outside heralded the arrival of more Priestmen. Villane darted back behind the door, motioning to Ruth to get down behind the nearest tier of pallets. York stationed himself to the left of Villane and Rourke and Jimmy crouched down out of sight next to the wall.

Amid the yellow flurry that came blasting through the door, was one red robe. Villane recognized Pume and, acting on an almost biological impulse, he reached out and grabbed him and pulled him from the midst of the startled Priestmen. He dragged Pume out into the middle of the floor, holding his arm twisted behind his back. He pointed his gun at the Priestmen. "Your Supreme Priestmen is now my Supreme Prisoner," he told them, his words slicing through his clenched teeth.

Pume struggled, crying out to the Priestmen to do something, to save him.

Before they could make up their minds or move, York, Jimmy and Rourke were among them, striking like cobras, yelling like lions. Sound shots scattered. Jimmy, hit, fell. As his dying body reached the floor, his eyes began to glaze and look away to another distant place that he was seeing for the first time.

They took the Priestmen's guns and pointed them like accusing fingers at them. Following Villane's orders, the Priestmen lined up against the wall, their eyes on Pume and on their own guns that had escaped the prisons of their hands.

"Pume," Villane demanded, "where are all the people?"

"Here," Pume answered. 'There." He pointed to the pallets where the citizens still reclined, undisturbed by the scene and the noise that surrounded them.

"I thought so," Villane said, releasing Pume. "Aren't you proud of what you've accomplished, Pume? Of what you've made of Cityside? You and your Priestmen have turned your world into a morgue!"

"They're alive!" Pume protested, failing completely to understand Villane's point.

"You call that living?" Villane indicated the rhythmically rising and falling chests of the citizens reclining in their pallets that looked so much like coffins.

Pume seemed to shrink inside himself. "They needed rest and recreation. I—we—did our best. The circus—Sensory Central—"

Villane turned from him in disgust. "York, get to the Dump. Destroy the dome."

York sprinted from the room.

"Ruth, you can come out now," Villane called. When she had joined him, he told Rourke, "Put our friends the Priestmen in one of the outer rooms and lock the door. I'll cover you and keep an eye on Pume at the same time." He stepped aside so that the long hall outside the open door was within his line of vision. Then, turning back to Pume, he asked, "Where are the rest of the Priestmen?"

Pume shook his head. "There aren't any others. They're all there."

Villane looked in the direction Pume had pointed—at the pallets. So, he thought, the Priestmen couldn't take Cityside either.

"Might's right," Pume murmured distractedly. "All's swell that works well. We did our best. There was always Landsend. We had to *survive!*"

Villane disregarded the wave of pity that washed over him as he listened to Pume rave on as he heard the walls of his world cracking and the sky falling in sickening shreds about his shoulders. "You're worse than a fool, Pume," Villane told him sadly. "You're a man with only one idea!"

Rourke returned and Villane sent him after Grandsir and the others. He stood, after Rourke had gone, with Ruth while Pume sat slumped, a puddle of flesh, on the floor at their feet, occasionally muttering what might have been words.

"Here, take this gun, Ruth and keep an eye on Pume. I'll be right back."

Villane walked purposefully to the nearest pallet and

kicked the spinning spool loose. He ripped the pins from the skin of the man lying on the pallet. Up and down the rows he went, repeating his action until not a spool remained whole nor a pin embedded in a body. The citizens rose up and moaned. They cried out for their bright lands and lost dreams. They milled about helplessly and wept and were afraid to go outside.

Grandsir came. Sister was with him. "We couldn't make the Landsenders come out," he told Villane.

"None of them would," Sister piped. "They're still sort of scared. Rourke's with them."

Villane said, "They'll come out. In time. As soon as we convince them that there is nothing left in Cityside to fear."

"You sure of that, boy?" Grandsir asked.

"I'm sure. Grandsir, I've got a job for you." Villane told him what he wanted him to do and Grandsir happily obliged. He began herding a group of people out of Sensory Central and down the steps to the street.

Villane said to Ruth, "Ever since the day I quit the Life Lab, I've been worrying and wondering about alternatives. Now I'm about to propose a few."

"Alternatives to what?" Ruth wanted to know.

"To Cityside. To circuses and Sensory Central. It's pretty simple, the way I see it. If reality—the reality that was Cityside, for example—is impossible to tolerate, the answer doesn't lie in withdrawal from that reality. It lies instead in *alternatives* to that reality. We have to create a new and different reality."

"We've already started to," Ruth said.

"Yes."

"No, you don't understand what I mean, Phillip." She patted her slightly rounded stomach. "Part of it is here. I'm pregnant."

Villane stared at her. Then he drew her to him and held her close, neither of them speaking for a long moment.

Pume got up and ambled aimlessly about the room, mumbling. They watched him go out the door and down the steps and stand dismayed as Grandsir passed, guiding his band of people past the building, their arms loaded with bombs, Sister frisking along beside them,

"They're going to bury them," Villane told Ruth. "They're going to defuse all the bombs and then they're going to put them down below the earth where they belong and they're going to bring the Landsenders up out of the earth and into the sunlight where *they* belong."

"Poor Pume," Ruth said, as she watched him wander away, his mind literally sickened by what he saw taking place before his eyes, a sight he found it impossible to comprehend.

"Let's go," Villane said. "We've got a lot to do. We've got to reeducate both the Landsenders and the Citysiders, scrub the earth clean out there, start curing the diseases the biobombs caused. We've got to find a way to take care of the Limbos and we've got to deactivate the heat field once and for all."

Ruth sighed and said, "I feel as if we've averted the death of earth and all its people. I feel good!"

Suddenly, the sky overhead tilted crazily and the sun spun in its fake orbit. Gradually, as Villane and Ruth watched, the dome rolled back and disappeared to reveal a new and much brighter sun sailing in the bluest sky either of them had ever seen.

"York's done it!" Villane shouted happily. His cry was matched by the joyous shouts of the bands of men he had dispatched earlier as they converged now in front of Sensory Central.

"Hey there, you two!" Grandsir called up to Villane and Ruth. "Did I ever tell you about snow? It's great!"

"I'll just bet it is!" Villane yelled back. He and Ruth walked down the steps together, not into Cityside, but into the one world that was big enough for everyone. The disks, relics of their past, gleamed above their left ears while within Ruth, new life stirred, a promise for their future.

THE END

FREE BOOKS!

Choose any 4 exciting Belmont Books listed below and receive the fifth book absolutely free! Choose 7 books and get 2 additional books free!

- ☐ **NOVELETS OF SCIENCE FICTION**, James Blish, Arthur C. Clarke, others
  A collection of SF gems, by Clifford Simak, Milton Lesser, Poul Anderson, etc.
  #B50-770, 50¢
- ☐ **WORLDS WITHOUT END**, by Clifford Simak
  Never before in book form, three masterful stories from one of the greatest writers of terror and science fiction. #B50-791, 50¢
- ☐ **A PIECE OF MARTIN CANN**, by Laurence M. Janifer
  All laws of science and medicine are changed; now we enter the minds and bodies of our patients and we too are changed, utterly . . . #B50-811, 50¢
- ☐ **THE LIVING DEMONS**, by Robert Bloch
  Monstrous creatures swarm beyond the boundaries of their nightmare world.
  #B50-787, 50¢
- ☐ **TIME UNTAMED**, anthology
  ★8★ amazing science fiction tales first time in paperback by all time greats—Isaac Asimov, Robert Bloch, Ray Bradbury, Clifford D. Simak, John Wyndham, Theodore Sturgeon, L. Sprague de Camp, and Fritz Leiber. #B50-781, 50¢
- ☐ **SPECIAL DELIVERY / STAR GLADIATOR**, by Kris Neville / Dave Van Arnam
  Two alien races battle for an unwary earth . . . How long can a lone man survive the brutality of 50 worlds? Two complete full length novels.
  #B50-788, 50¢
- ☐ **AFTER SOME TOMORROW**, by Mack Reynolds
  A world could be changed by ESP, but only if a man wanted to risk everything.
  #B50-795, 50¢
- ☐ **THE COUNTERFEITS**, by Leo F. Kelley
  It was business as usual on earth and no one suspected the sky held something more than the sun, the moon and the stars. #B50-797, 50¢
- ☐ **TOWER AT THE EDGE OF TIME**, by Lin Carter
  What strange powers thrust the warrior and two men of greed into the limbo beyond time? #B50-804, 50¢
- ☐ **THE THIEF OF THOTH**, by Lin Carter
  Does crime pay—if a galaxy is the prize?
  AND OTHERS SHALL BE BORN, by Frank Belknap Long
  Not quite human . . . not quite alien—but inexplicably dangerous.
  #B50-809, 50¢
- ☐ **ASYLUM EARTH**, by Bruce Eliot
  The unseen but deadly battle between the world of no time and no place . . . and the here and now of Earth. #B50-819, 50¢
- ☐ **THE NON-STATISTICAL MAN**, by Raymond F. Jones
  One man's mind spins a taut and eerie arc from the dark past into the distant future and suddenly the world looks different. #B50-820, 50¢
- ☐ **EARTH UNAWARE**, by Mack Reynolds
  His unearthly power could destroy the world—was there no one to stop him?
  #B50-826, 50¢
- ☐ **ODYSSEY TO EARTHDEATH**, by Leo P. Kelley
  Death is the only answer to war. #B60-085, 60¢
- ☐ **SPACE TUG**, by Murray Leinster
  A startling science fiction novel of our country's desperate attempt to supply our men living on the moon. #B50-846, 50¢

Order from your bookseller, if sold out use this special price coupon.

Belmont Books, Dept. 085
1116 First Avenue, New York, N.Y. 10021

Please send me the books I have checked above: Any five 50¢ books for $2.00. (One book FREE.) Nine 50¢ books for $3.50. (Two books FREE.) Two 60¢ books for $1.00. Single copies list price plus 10¢ postage.

Name..

Address...

City........................State.............Zip Code............